Herbert Vivian

The green bay tree

A tale of to-day

Herbert Vivian

The green bay tree
A tale of to-day

ISBN/EAN: 9783337121426

Printed in Europe, USA, Canada, Australia, Japan

Cover: Foto ©Andreas Hilbeck / pixelio.de

More available books at **www.hansebooks.com**

The Green Bay Tree

A tale of to-day
by

W·H·WILKINS
(W·H·de WINTON)

Author of 'St Michael's Eve'
'The Forbidden Sacrifice' &c

AND

HERBERT VIVIAN

sometime editor of the 'Whirlwind'

LONDON 1894
HUTCHINSON & CO
34 Paternoster Row

PRINTED AT NIMEGUEN (HOLLAND)
BY H. C. A. THIEME OF NIMEGUEN (HOLLAND
AND
TALBOT HOUSE, ARUNDEL STREET
LONDON, W.C.

CONTENTS

PREFATORY NOTE

Chapters I, II, VI, VII, VIII, IX and X in this volume are written by MR. W. H. WILKINS.

Chapters III, IV, V, XI, XII and XIII are written by MR. HERBERT VIVIAN.

THE GREEN BAY TREE.

CHAPTER I.

THE CITY OF LES DOULEURS.

Lasciate ogni speranza
Voi ch'entrate
— DANTE, "INFERNO".

Les Douleurs, 'the City of Charlemagne' or, as the Pope has termed it, 'the City of the Saints'—though to the lay mind it would rather seem the City of the Sinners, and withal miserable sinners—looked very bright one morning in mid-July. It was early morning. There was just that touch of freshness in the air, which dies as the day wears on, and the dew was yet wet on the grass. The band was playing away merrily in the Kiosk, and the

shady little Elisen Garden—the spot where visitors
most do congregate—was thronged with Cure-guests,
who had risen betimes to drink in draughts of
health from the healing springs.

It was a motley crowd of half the peoples, nations,
and languages under heaven. Russians, Germans,
Dutch, French, Americans, English, Belgians, all
jostled one against another as they ascended and
descended the steep stone steps which led to the
Elisen brunnen—all clamouring for their water and
taxing to their utmost the energies of the blue-eyed
maiden, who was the presiding genius of these
sulphurous libations.

If one wished to study types, one could hardly
do better than go to the Elisen Garden on this
fine morning. There was an English Duchess, who,
(as she explained to an acquaintance who had turned
up unexpectedly) had been sent by her doctor to
Aix-les-Bains, but came here by mistake. Why
she did not remedy the error by packing up and

departing by the next train, it is not easy to see. There was a thick-lipped Russian Prince who, rumour said, had incurred the displeasure of his Imperial Master and was, apparently, whiling away his banishment by coming here, to dip and be clean, like Naaman of old in Jordan. There was a besotted English peer, accompanied by a muscular music-hall *artiste*. They were passing themselves off, these two, as 'Mr. and Mrs. Smith' and were fondly deluding themselves that the incognito was respected. There was a colonial Archdeacon, who button-holed everyone to explain that he was here for his rheumatism, as though anyone cared whether he had rheumatism or not. There was quite a crowd of young Englishmen—in the Service for the most part—from Henrion's and Dremel's Hotels, and there was a prizefighter and a third-rate Gaiety actress. Altogether it was a remarkable variety-show and differed from other watering-places in Europe mainly in two respects—the scarcity of its old women, and the number of its young men.

Two of these young men, Englishmen obviously, were pacing round the shingly path of the Elisen Garden, keeping unconscious time with the music of the band. One of them, a good-looking youth with a dark clear-cut face, was carefully dressed in a suit of fresh, neat flannels, with the regulation brown-leather boots and cool straw hat. He walked along with an easy step, the embodiment of superb health and careful grooming, he looked as if he had never known a care. His companion had a dejected appearance and a lacklustre eye; his clothes were loosely huddled on as though he had jumped out of bed in a hurry, and was not quite awake even now. His face was unshaven, and altogether he had a very washed-out appearance. In his hand he carried a glass of tepid water, which he sipped every now and then with an expression of intense disgust.

"This is the third glass of this beastly stuff I

have got down," he exclaimed presently. " One more yet—'must have four', the doctor says. Ugh! I wish he had to drink it himself, and then perhaps he wouldn't be so free with prescribing it to other people."

" Considering you have come all this way for the purpose, it would be rather a disappointment if he didn't dose you, wouldn't it?" asked Coryton, switching at a lime leaf with his cane.

" It's a beastly hole to come to anyway," growled Tyrconnel. " Let me see, how long have we been here, Corry? Three weeks, I think. It will be my twenty-first bath to-day. It must be jolly slow for you, old chap, with no cure to fill up the time."

" Thanks—very good of you to think of me, I am sure," replied the other with a curious smile, " but I think on the whole I prefer my leisure and am content to leave you the cure."

" Well, it's awfully good of you to have come with me. I don't know what I should have done without you—committed suicide I think in very melancholy madness. You are the best friend I have in the world. No other fellow would have stood by me as you have done and followed me to this infernal hole——"

" I would do anything for you Tyrconnel, you know that—go through fire and water if need be."

This is a sort of acrobatic performance, which is always being volunteered by people who would hesitate to lend one a ten-pound note; Tyrconnel did not know that. Just now he believed in Coryton more than ever. Had he not stood up for him against his father, had he not thrown up a yachting trip to join him here? True, the yachting trip was somewhat *in nubibus*, and Coryton was quartered for six weeks in one of the best hotels with all expenses paid, and handsome *baksheesh* in his pocket from Lord Baltinglass of Blarney besides, as a small return for all the wise counsel and good advice he had given to his prodigal son.

'That is a very clever young fellow,—a man who'll make a name in the world, you mark my words if he doesn't. Just the sort of friend Wilfrid should have," remarked Lord Baltinglass one evening after dinner to his elderly maiden sister, who presided over his house—or rather houses—for him. Coryton had sat at his feet all the evening, applauding his opinions, laughing at his jokes, treating him with an exquisite deference, which insinuated that it was on Baltinglass, and Baltinglass alone that the future of the House of Lords and the consequent safety of the Empire depended.

Lord Baltinglass's sister, Miss Kezia Tyrconnel, *née* Simpson, a lady of evangelical views, with whom Coryton had discussed the future of Protestantism in the Church of England in the interval after tea, entirely agreed.

"Ah! If Wilfrid were only more like him! Young men are so careless about religion nowadays," she sighed, shaking her ringlets. "By the way have you noticed, Baltinglass, how ill Wilfrid is looking? And his cough troubles him a good deal too. I am afraid he is going just like his poor dear mother."

Miss Tyrconnel sighed again. She was given to gloomy forebodings. She called it 'going to the bottom of things.'

"Dear me," cried Lord Baltinglass in alarm, " You don't say so."

This allusion to his wife's decease frightened him. He remembered how she had pined away amid her uncongenial surroundings, a prey to an insidious disease. Consumptive tendencies were hereditary to the Tyrconnel family.

" What's to be done ? " he asked blankly.

" I have already asked the Reverend Fyre Irons to offer supplication for him to the Throne of Grace," replied Miss Tyrconnel piously, " and I need scarcely say that I too supplicate both night and morning."

She folded her hands and cast her eyes upward with the air of one who would say, " What can poor mortal do more? "

Lord Baltinglass gave an impatient snort.

" He must consult Dr. Doublefee without delay," he said.

So Dr. Doublefee was consulted, and the upshot was that that eminent physician advised a course of the waters of *Les Douleurs*. It was Coryton who travelled up to town with his friend and penetrated with him into Doublefee's Holy of Holies. It was Coryton who suggested that Wilfrid should not go alone to a foreign land. It was Coryton who slipped into his waistcoat pocket, after many protests, the handsome cheque of a grateful parent.

Such touching devotion almost made Miss Tyrconnel shed tears.

" It quite reminds me of David and Jonathan," she whimpered at parting " or those two heathen creatures—I quite forget their names—one used to read about them in Miss Medgeworth's Mythology revised for family and domestic reading."

"Nisus and Euryalus," suggested Coryton.

Miss Tyrconnel did not hear him. She was tugging something from her pocket.

"Dear Mr. Coryton," she said, "You must accept this little gift from me—oh yes, you really must—in memory of our many solemn talks on holy things."

Coryton took the little package. Could it be Bank notes? It felt soft. There was no time to examine it closely then. But when later on in the train he opened it to find nothing but a morocco bound edition of 'Saved from the Pit, or The Sinner's Refuge,' he threw it out of the window with an oath which would have made the estimable giver's ringlets stand forth like 'the quills of the fretful porcupine', could she have heard it.

"I don't know how I shall hold out for the

six weeks. I feel awfully bad already," resumed Tyrconnel presently, as he tackled his fourth glass of water. "I can eat nothing."

"Well, you must take a turn on omelettes, like the other fellows," said Coryton consolingly. "They cook an omelette better than anything else here, and they ought to do so, considering what a run there is on them. Cheer up, old chap, 'it might be worse,' as a man once remarked who looked into Hades and saw the Devil carrying off his friend."

"I don't quite see how it could be worse than that," said the other ruefully.

"Well, his friend might have had to carry the Devil," rejoined Coryton drily. "But let us turn round the other way, here's Wrigglesworth bearing down upon us. You don't want to know him, I think you said."

"No, he's such a malicious old brute, he abuses everyone."

" Well, there is no advantage in not knowing him, so far as that is concerned, for he abuses a stranger just as much as a friend—the only difference is that he draws on his imagination a little more. However, we are safe from him now, he has swooped down upon the Archdeaconess, who is perched as usual on her little seat in the corner. Poor woman! I pity her. Let us go a little nearer the band. I want to hear this Brahms' *Liebes Lieder* Waltz .... By Jove! Pigeon," he exclaimed, suddenly catching his friend by the arm, " Do you see who is coming along? Sally Popkins! By all that's wonderful——"

Sally it was beyond a doubt, wearing an innocent white gown and sailor hat, with a red parasol in her hand, tripping straight towards them smiling as the morn. Tyrconnel flushed hotly and would have turned aside, but before he could do so, Sally was upon them.

" Well, I never!" she exclaimed, twirling her

parasol round like a vast butterfly, "who would
have thought of meeting you here? How are you,
Mr. Coryton? No need to ask. And you Mr.
Tyrconnel? pretty fit, I hope. Surely you haven't
forgotten me. What, not very well? I am *so*
sorry. You do look rather sorry for yourself, I
must say."

"The morning light is trying even to the best
complexions, Miss Popkins," interposed Coryton.
"What brings you here, I wonder?"

"Rheumatism, of course," cried Sally with a
rippling laugh, "I was sent to Aix-les-Bains and
came to this place by mistake—that's the thing
to say, I hear. No, the fact was I came over
to see a friend of mine, Pussie Prancewell. She
used to dance at the Gaiety, you know—I wanted a
little holiday and thought I might as well come
here. Do you know Pussie? She's great fun."

"I believe I saw her taking the dust on the road
beyond Burtscheid yesterday," said Coryton.

" It doesn't seem a bad sort of place," said Sally, twirling her parasol and glancing coyly at the Russian Prince. " I am told it's poor fun to come here, but people seem to enjoy themselves anyway."

" What would you have them do ?" queried Coryton, with an amused smile. " There is such a thing as 'Happiness in Hell', some people say. What— going, Tyrconnel? Well, I must be going too. Ta-ta, Miss Popkins, see you later, I hope....."

" Why are you so glum, old chap?" he asked of Tyrconnel presently, as they walked together down the narrow uneven pavement of the Büchel on the way back to Dubigk's Hotel, "Aren't you pleased to see Sally?"

" Pleased !" echoed the other indignantly. " How can you ask me? Doesn't it remind me of the most discreditable incident of my life? Corry, I feel that that woman is my evil genius—a sort of Circe, who turns all who come near her into swine. She is to me the embodiment of the lowest part of one's nature. You needn't sneer, I mean it."

"We all mean these admirable sentiments—the first thing in the morning. If we only acted upon them in the evening, what a different world it would be. Don't turn away from me, old chap. I was only joking. You know that. I can't cure myself of the habit. But, joking apart, though, I think you take matters too seriously. We all have our own little peccadilloes. Even St. Augustine was a rake in his youth—that is why he became a saint later, I suppose. But as to poor little Sally, you are too hard on her, 'pon my word. She is just like all the rest of her kind, neither better nor worse—rather better, for she is distinctly amusing, which is something in a world made up for the most part of the bores and the bored. Altogether, I am not sorry she has turned up. She will help us to pass the time here and we can have some fun together. Won't we?"

"No," said Tyrconnel doggedly, "I won't. No more paltering with temptation for me."

Coryton gave him a quick glance. They were under the colonnade of the *Kurhaus* now, just turning into the hotel. The shadow was so great he could scarcely see his companion's face, which was bent towards the ground. But he saw that the usually mobile lips were close shut. It would not do to press him further.

"My dear fellow," he said in a tone of real feeling, linking his arm in his, "You are perfectly right, it will be best for you to give the siren a wide berth. We will say no more about it. Come and let us have our breakfast out in the garden; the letters must have come by now."

They took their breakfast, a frugal meal after the manner of German breakfasts—just a trout, fragrant coffee, crisp fresh rolls, and golden honey —on the vine-clad balcony which overlooks the quaint old garden of Dubigk's delightful hotel.

Conversation languished somewhat, as it is apt to do the first thing in the morning, especially with people who have reached a stage of intimacy, which renders it unnecessary. The head waiter came presently with a bundle of newspapers and letters. Coryton's were soon disposed of; they were bills and duns principally, forwarded from his Jermyn-Street lodgings; one a County Court summons inclosed in a registered letter, a new form of torture invented to plague unfortunate debtors. He smiled grimly and tore it into little shreds, making a little orange-hued heap on his plate.

"Well, I am out of the way over here at any rate," he thought to himself.

Then he scanned the "Fashionable Intelligence" column in yesterday's morning paper, chiefly so called because it contains intelligence about people who are not fashionable, but who cheerfully pay their guinea a line to be thought so by suburban acquaintances and country cousins. Beyond an announcement that a marriage was arranged between Mr. Plantagenet-Unkels of Kensington-beyond-Jordan and Miss Verity of Bayswater-by-Whiteley, it contained nothing which had even the faintest semblance of interest to him. So he looked idly across at his companion.

Tyrconnel's under-lip was quivering and his eyes were big with suspicious moisture. He was reading over, for the third or fourth time, a letter of several sheets written in a thin, firm handwriting. Coryton's brow contracted a little, as he recognized the handwriting. It was Gwendolen's.

Tyrconnel looked up, and their eyes met.

"It is a letter from Gwendolen," he faltered. "I couldn't help it, Corry. I felt so wretched and miserable. I was obliged to write to her and she—has answered. What a brute I feel! I have broken her heart."

"Hearts, which break, break in silence," said Coryton, with a thin vein of contempt in his voice.

"They do not relieve themselves on six closely written pages of foreign note."

"I do not mean that." cried the other indignantly. "Gwen is far too noble-minded to speak of her own sufferings. but one can read between the lines. Not a word of reproach for all I have done—not one word! Do you think she will ever take me back again?"

Coryton took a cigarette from his case before replying. He lit it and looked across at Herr Henrion's pigeons sunning themselves on the red-tiled roof. He seemed lost in thought.

"Do you?" persisted Tyrconnel.

Coryton blew a thin cloud of blue smoke into the summer air. From the other side of the court, he could hear Miss Gussie Gutter, the music-hall singer, croaking out the fragment of a familiar melody, as she made ready for her bath.

"Oh! what a difference in the morning
What an alteration in the dawning!"

He waited until the verse was finished before replying. Then he said in his blandest accents,

"My dear fellow, how can I possibly answer for a girl like Gwendolen Haviland? She and I approach everything from a different point of view, and besides you haven't shown me her letter yet. In the old days they used to kill the fatted calf for the prodigal; now they rather slam the door in his face. I mean your good religious people, not—*nous autres*. Ah! is that the letter? Thanks."

"Take you back? I should think she would," he continued presently, "it is evident in every line. Even if it were not, Mrs. de Courcy Miles would see to it. But the question is, do you wish to go back? Remember, she never knew the details, and she treated you very hardly, I thought. What was there in your being sent down to make her throw you over as she did? Many good men and true have been sent down before. If she had really cared for you, she wouldn't have done it."

"Oh! but you don't know Gwen," broke in the other eagerly, "how pure she is, how good, how noble. She loves me, but there is One Whom she loves more still. You smile, Coryton. I am not over religious, I know, but I do believe— in Gwendolen. She sees things through other eyes than ours. She does not know the details, you say,—she must never know them—never—*never*. But you do not know all. Only two days before that—that Cottenham dinner, she had given herself to me, her pure, sweet love—all she had; and I—I had vowed to lead a better life for her sake. And then, with my vows still ringing in her ears, she heard that—I had been sent down. Could she forgive—how could she believe in me longer? So, as you know, she broke it all off—and I—I don't know how I have lived since then, drifting about like a rudderless ship. So I wrote to her at last,—to plead for one more chance, and this is her answer. Tell me, Corry, what does she mean?"

"She means, if I know anything about such things," Coryton replied, tossing back the letter, "that she is at present fighting a battle between her inclination and what she conceives to be her duty."

"And you think——?"

"That her inclination will conquer, of course. It always does. She will take you back, Pigeon, never fear. This is merely fencing before the buttons are off the foils."

"What do you advise me to do?—I cannot go on like this."

"My dear fellow, I advise you to do whatever you think you wish to do. I have a theory that people only take advice which happens to fit in with their inclinations."

Tyrconnel thought a moment, then a flash illumined his eyes.

"I know what I will do," he said. "I will ask Aunt Kezia to write to Mrs. de Courcy Miles and get her to bring Gwen to Blarney in September, when you and Vixie will be there. When we are together once more, she will relent, I am sure she will — but——" His face suddenly fell. "Do you think she will consent to come?"

"Mrs. de Courcy Miles will see to that," replied Coryton with a moody laugh.

So Gwendolen and Tyrconnel would come together after all! Well, it would be best to recognize the situation and bow to the inevitable. "*Che sarà sarà*," he muttered between his teeth.

"What did you say?" queried Tyrconnel, looking up from the letter he was now reading for a fourth time.

"Merely that it is best to recognize the inevitable in all things.—Ah! there goes Sally Popkins with the Russian Prince, as I live. Why, they didn't know one another half an hour ago! But she knows how to improve the shining hour, does Sally."

"She does indeed," said Tyrconnel with an

expression of disgust. "Talk about the inevitable—
it seems inevitable for that woman to cross my
path—and just now too, of all times. I believe there
is destiny in it."

"Destiny," rejoined Coryton, "bah! Destiny does
not concern itself with insignificant atoms like
you and me. Do not let us lay that flattering
unction to our souls. We are creatures of chance,
blown hither and thither like straws before the
wind."

"Gwendolen would not say so," replied Tyrconnel returning to his letter.

"Gwendolen!" echoed Coryton with an evil smile.

Then he sprang from his chair impatiently.

"Nearly ten o'clock. Isn't it about time for
you to have your sulphurous bath, Tyrconnel?
Now don't be so down in the mouth. This fine
weather ought to affect you like a barometer. You
ought to be up I don't know where, instead of
persistently remaining below Zero. Come, we'll

stroll across to the Rosenbad together. We'll toss
those little green frogs we bought in the Fels-
gasse yesterday, over into the other people's baths.
Won't Gussie Gutter yell? Of course I shall swear
that you did it. Come, Joseph must have been waiting
an age. In the afternoon we'll walk over to Vals
and see Thérèse."

He linked his arm in Tyrconnel's and they
walked over to the long low building the other
side of the road, yclept the Rosenbad. As they
pushed open the doors, an odour anything but
rose-like greeted their nostrils, the sulphurous
fumes, with which the place was impregnated,
forcibly suggesting the pit of Tophet. In the
covered hall at the back and in the little triangular
garden there were a good many people sitting or
standing about, patiently or impatiently waiting
their turn. The bath-accommodation at Les Douleurs
is absurdly limited, considering the number of
visitors who seek its healing springs.

Tyrconnel and his companion, however, had not long to wait. They possessed, or rather one of them did—that golden key, which unlocks all doors. The perspiring Joseph greeted them with an obsequious smile and bowed them down to the white marble baths, reserved for them at the end of a very long, narrow passage.

Coryton's tub was a simple matter. As he was not going in for the cure, it was soon over. So when he had leisurely dressed in the dainty blue and white chamber leading from the steps of his bath, he brought out of his pocket the box of little frogs, which he had smuggled in with him and prepared for action. The baths at the Rosenbad run along in a row adjoining one another. They are each separated by high tiled walls, which form separate little bath-rooms, but all are open to the lofty dome-like roof.

Coryton listened, the spirit of mischief in his eyes. Every bath seemed full along the line and

from nearly all came whistling, humming, or snatches
of song, with which the bathers are wont to dispel
the bad half-hour, during which they sit up to their
chins in the greenish yellow water. He could hear
some little way down, Miss Gussie Gutter crooning:

" Wot cher 'Ria?
'Ria's on the job."

and nearer a volatile Frenchman's truculent:

" *Malbrou' s'en va-t-en guerre,*
Miron-ton-ton ton, mirontaine;
Qui sait quand reviendra?"

while just beyond Tyrconnel's bath there came a
grunting :

" *Hopp, hopp, hopp*
Pferdchen lauf' Galopp,
Über Stock und über Steine
Aber brich mir nicht die Beine!
Immer im Gallopp,
Hopp, hopp, hopp, hopp!"

from a fat old German Countess.

" Hist! Pigeon," whispered Coryton tapping the
wall, which divided them. " Now!"

The songs suddenly ceased. There came a volley

of shrill Billingsgate from the fair Gussie, an exasperated '*Scrongnieu!*' from the Frenchman, a guttural '*Donnerwetter!*' from the German Countess, a violent ringing of bells, a rushing to and fro of attendants, and exclamations of reprimand, disgust, and indignation all along the line.

The author of all the trouble strolled out with an impassive countenance and, meeting the angry Frau Lincter (the presiding genius of the Rosenbad,) gave a significant nod in the direction of Tyrconnel's bath.

CHAPTER II.

A CURE-HOUSE REVEL.

Vado a balar ze vero
Cossa ghe ze de mal?
Saltar a l'età mia
No l'è pecà mortal.
Se gira e se se sburta
E se se fa strucar
Vado a balar ze vero
No steme a tormentar.
—VENETIAN SONG.

CORYTON paused for a moment uncertainly as the glass doors of the bath-house swung to behind him. Then he bent his steps in the direction of Mariahilf, and strolled leisurely up to the Lousberg.

It was a beautiful day, bright and clear, the

gardens of the villas in Ludwig's Allée were all a-bloom, and the lime-trees swung their fragrant censers low above his head as he walked along. But he hardly noticed it all. His face was dark, and his thoughts were occupied with other things.

What brought this moody cloud to his brow?

Coryton had hoped to play off Sally upon Tyrconnel, against Gwendolen. What he expected to gain out of it all was hardly clear even to himself. He only knew that with Gwendolen's influence in the ascendant, he would gain nothing. And when Gwendolen broke with Tyrconnel after he had been sent down from Cambridge, it seemed as though he had succeeded. But when he found that Tyrconnel was writing to Gwendolen behind his back, he was shrewd enough to see that the game was up. It was no use opposing him. There was a strong vein of obstinacy in Tyrconnel's character and Coryton, who knew this, felt that the only thing was to play to his likings; and since his mind was set on Gwendolen, he would marry her. But the marriage must be brought about in such a way that it would seem that it was through Coryton—and Coryton alone—that it came to pass. And after?

"Well," he thought with a cynical smile, "one must wait the progress of events, a disillusion may set in. More love dies from satiety than from starvation. It is impossible to interest, or to be interested in, a person one sees every day."

The future, however, was uncertain. One thing only was certain now, and that was, that Sally was played out—at any rate for the present. Tyrconnel evidently viewed her with aversion as the origin of all his troubles.

Coryton thought of all this as he climbed the steep ascent. The Lousberg is a curving, pyramid-shaped hill which rises abruptly out of the plain. Fifty years ago it was bleak and naked, but now with its shady avenues and winding walks, it forms a sort of Bois de Boulogne to Les Douleurs. Coryton went up as far as the Josephine Monument, and leaning over the railing looked down upon the city stretched out panorama-wise beneath. His gaze wandered over the octagon-shaped dome of Charlemagne's famous Cathedral, past the Marschier gate and the old ivy-covered fortifications, to where the Eifel mountains loomed a broad line of blue on the distant horizon. He was all alone. The place seemed deserted. It was yet the forenoon and most of the visitors were occupied with their cure. By and by, when the band played in the Belvedere just below where he was standing, it would be crowded, and still more thronged to-morrow evening, for the *Fremden-Blatt* had announced fireworks on the Lousberg, and the Salvator church on the hill opposite was to be illuminated by the white glare of electric light.

A great wave of bitterness swept over Coryton as he stood gazing over the wide champaign; a sense of the injustice of things arose in his heart, as he contrasted his own position with that of Tyrconnel's.

"Here am I," he thought, "with ability and energy enough for ten men"—he was not prone to underrate himself—"and every promise of success, were not every promise blasted by the lack of opportunity which money alone brings. While this raw youth with but a fraction of my brains, has only to stretch out his hand and all good things are showered into it. Wealth, fame, power, gratified ambition—all may be his. While—I—I am never to have a fair chance. I am to be content to black his boots—to be grateful for the crumbs which fall from the rich man's table—to end life at the point at which he started.

He beat his hand against the railings in the agony of his hate and scorn.

"Is it a wonder," he continued to himself, "that I am driven into crooked and tortuous paths, to plot and scheme with sharpers and *cocottes*, when these things are so? What chance have I otherwise?—Oh yes, it is easy to practise all the virtues—when one has a good balance at one's bankers—the poor man cannot afford them. It is better to be born blind, and deaf, and lame than without money. Neither heaven nor earth have any good for those who have it not. Gad! When I think of it all, the game of living seems hardly worth the candle."

We have all our weak moments, even the wisest among us.

He was so engrossed with his thoughts that he did not hear a light step behind him falling softly on the grass. Someone tapped him on the shoulder, and a high-pitched voice, cried:

" Well, old chappie, what are you thinking about so hard? "

Coryton swerved round and faced Sally (for she it was) with all the evil passions his thoughts had called up marked upon his face. Try as he would, he could not obliterate them in a moment. He wanted to be alone just now, and she jarred upon him. Besides, he had no use for her at present.

"I was thinking,"—he said shortly, after a moment's pause, "of Charlemagne."

"Charlie who?" flippantly rejoined the irrepressible Sally. "Don't know him. Is he a friend of yours?"

Then she sat down on a bench with her back to the view and swung her heels together. She had no eye for the beauties of nature, it appeared.

"It's lucky we have met, for I have been wanting to have a talk with you," she continued. "Come now, you needn't give yourself those high-and-mighty airs."

Coryton ignored the latter part of the speech,—in fact he scarcely heard it. He was trying to bring his emotions under control, and well-disciplined though they were, it was a minute or so before he could manage to do so. He looked down, and began to punch little holes in the turf with his stick.

"What is it you want?" he asked at last.

"Oof!" replied Sally laconically, bringing her heels together with a click.

"I hope you may get it," rejoined Coryton indifferently. "You won't get any out of me. You ought to know that by this time. Dog doesn't eat dog you know."

Then he went on digging at the turf again.

A little flush of annoyance crept over Sally's well-powdered cheeks.

"There's the Pigeon," she said tentatively. "What about him?" Her voice became a trifle shriller.

"The Pigeon's no go," answered Coryton with a short laugh, "he has eaten sour grapes and his teeth are set on edge. No more cakes and ale for the Pigeon. He is going to marry and mend his ways. The game's up, my dear Miss de Vere, so far as he is concerned. You had better seek fresh fields and pastures new. You'll get nothing more out of that particular pasture, I warrant you."

"I never did get anything out of it," cried Sally jumping up indignantly from her seat. "Nothing at all, I never saw him after that evening,—you know that; and I nearly had a row with Pimlico into the bargain..... So this is the end of all your fine promises, is it? You may be a very clever fellow, Mr. Coryton—so I daresay you are— for yourself—but you won't catch me doing any more of your dirty work in a hurry, I can tell you."

She faced him with flashing eyes, her voice rising almost to the upper C. These moods did not suit Sally. In them the artificial veneer was apt to wear off, to reveal the coarse grains underneath.

Coryton shrugged his shoulders at the ebullition. His face was inscrutable. He had got the mastery over himself by this time.

"Isn't it rather a pity to waste so much energy?"
he said quietly. "If you scream so loud all Aix
will hear you."

"I don't care if they do," retorted Sally crescendo:
"I have a good mind to go to Tyrconnel and
tell him the whole story."

"Do you think he would believe a word you
said?" replied Coryton contemptuously. "But
come, let us drop these heroics; they don't become
you and they bore me. Granted this little affair
has turned out a failure. Whose fault is it? Not
mine, I assure you.... I have put you on many
good things before now and may do so again—if
you only keep cool. Gratitude, we both understand,
means a keen sense of favours to come; there will
be more favours, believe me, if only you are
reasonable and do as I tell you."

"That's all very fine," retorted Sally, a little
mollified none the less. "A bird in the hand's
worth two in the bush. I might believe you if

I saw the colour of your coin. It would prove you were in earnest," she added coaxingly; " come, put a tenner now."

" You'll never get a brass farthing out of me," rejoined Coryton brutally. " I'm too wary a bird to buy off my Danes.... You don't grasp the allusion? Well, never mind. It only means there's no cash in this quarter. There's the Russian Prince, why not try him?—or old Colonel Oldbags of the Blues? A tenner forsooth! What's the good of a tenner. I can put you up to a dodge by which we'll get not a tenner—but hundreds, not just yet perhaps—but a little later, when the Pigeon has settled down in the odour of sanctity .... We cannot all pay for our youthful follies, you know. Come, let us walk down the hill together, and I will tell you how to work the oracle as we go along...."

Sally sulkily consented.

What transpired between them it is impossible

to say, but when Miss Popkins appeared in the
Kurhaus Garden the evening of the same day, her
good humour was apparently restored.

Perhaps it was that little luncheon with the
Russian Prince, which had most to do with it.
Anyway, she greeted Coryton with a smile in which
there was no trace of ill-will: for Tyrconnel was
reserved a saddened inclination of the head and a
sigh strangled in its birth. It was lost upon him,
however, for he was walking with the Archdeaconess.

That good lady, who was something of a perma-
nency at Les Douleurs, and whose little rooms in the
Büchel were quite a centre for the English Colony,
was busily engaged in pointing out to Tyrconnel
the local celebrities of the place. These mustered
in great force to-night, for it was the occasion
of what the *Kur-Verein* were pleased to denominate
a *Grande Réunion*—illuminations and a dance. The
dingy garden of the *Kurhaus*, by day hardly a
cheerful place, was on this particular evening trans-

formed into a fairyland; ropes of coloured lamps ran from end to end, and many hundred lanterns gleamed among the trees. Groups of people were gathered around the little tables, chatting and laughing as they drank their beer, (without which no German festivity would be complete), or were walking up and down, listening to the music of the band.

In the larger ball-room of the *Kurhaus* — a handsome room richly decorated with stuccoes and paintings, — another band was playing. The windows were wide open to the summer night, and through them at intervals streamed the dancers, pacing up and down the balcony and looking down therefrom at the animated scene below.

The Archdeaconess kept a tight hold on Tyrconnel, as she gave him sage advice as to whom to know and whom to avoid, and she listened sympathetically to his troubles the while — or at least to as much of them as he felt inclined to tell

her. She was one of the kindest-hearted of women—
with a weakness for young Englishmen. She never
forced confidences, but she heard a good many—
and very strange ones they must have been, some
of them.

"People often tell me more than they think,"
she would remark sagely over her cup of ʻ English ʼ
tea, and no doubt they did, for a prolonged sojourn
at Les Douleurs is apt to sharpen one's powers
of observation. Besides which, mothers confided
in her—those who knew her—and bade her give
an eye to their youthful prodigals. Miss Tyrconnel,
who had heard of her through her pastor, the Rev
Fyre Irons, who had once been chaplain here, had
written to her, imploring her to keep watch on
Wilfrid. She was just the person to do it. Was
she not the widow of an Archdeacon? Did she
not keep the keys of the Church?

"I must introduce you to the Chaplain's daughters,
Mr. Tyrconnel," she said as they walked round under

the trees, " such sweet girls—that was one of them,
Barbara, dancing just now with Baron von Stern."

" Rather a funny place for a chaplain to bring
his daughters, isn't it?" asked Tyrconnel blankly,
gazing round at the motley crowd.

The Archdeaconess laughed.

" Well, since you mention it," she replied confidentially, " it is; I should not have said anything myself,
but if they were *my* girls——" She gave her shoulders
an expressive shrug. " However, the Chaplain is a
very strange man. Did you hear of that dispute
he had the other day with Colonel Oldbags?"

"No, all I know of him is that he deals in
very bad cigars," rejoined Tyrconnel, who had a
vivid recollection of some vile 'Trichies,' which the
reverend gentleman palmed off upon him at a mark
a piece.

The Archdeaconess smiled broadly—a meaning
smile.

" Dear Mr. Tyrconnel, you don't mean to say he

has been trying that on with you already? I ought to have warned you. Why, that is a very old game. I know exactly what he said: Just a very few which he brought with him from India, —he would let you have an odd hundred as a very great favour. That was it, wasn't it? .... Ah! yes, I thought so. Brought them from India indeed! Why, he buys them down at Schmidt's, in the Fels-gasse, for five marks the gross, and then sells them at £5 a hundred. He ought to be ashamed of himself—quite a disgrace to the cloth I call it! But there—these ex-army chaplains! How different to the poor dear Archdeacon, or even that shepherd of souls Mr. Fyre Irons. However, Barbara is a sweet girl and dances so nicely. Shall we go up to the ball-room now? and I will introduce you."

"I shall be very glad to be introduced—but I can't dance—I don't feel up to it."

"Ah! those baths are very fatiguing," rejoined the Archdeaconess and then she squeezed his arm.

"I am *so* sorry for you—dear Mr. Tyrconnel, I have had sons of my own. But there, you have come to the right place to get well, Les Douleurs is perfectly wonderful. You have only had twenty-one I think you said. By the time your cure is over I hope to see you spinning round the room like a top. If you will wait just one moment I will leave my bonnet in the cloak-room, and we will go into the ball-room together."

The band was playing the sugary-sweet Danube Waltz as they entered the room, and a good many couples were revolving to its strains. There was a great variety of waltzing, the queer German *deuxtemps* steps being perhaps the most predominant, but there was also the Liverpool lurch, the Hampstead hop, the Clapham slide, and the Kensington-beyond-Jordan shuffle, for the sort of Englishmen who dance at Les Douleurs generally hail from some of these classic parts. The others are content to look on. There were a good many looking

on to-night, standing in groups far out into the
room so as to seriously interfere with the comfort
of the dancers. The Archdeaconess made her way
up to one of these groups.

"Dear Colonel Oldbags," she exclaimed, effusively
bearing down upon a battered young-elderly man
who was leaning against the wall. "So pleased
to see you again! When did you come? You are
staying at Nuellens as usual, I suppose?" Then
without waiting for an answer to these questions,
"Let me introduce Mr. Tyrconnel. . . . . . Colonel Oldbags is quite an *habitué* of Les Douleurs,"
she explained.

"You have been here before?" queried Tyrconnel by way of saying something, for Oldbags
regarded him in silence with a melancholy stare.

"Fifteen times," rejoined the Colonel with the
air of one who has done something to be proud
of—"three times every year for the last five years.
It has been my salvation. You remember"—turn-

ing to the Archdeaconess—" what a wreck I was when first I came and—look at me now."

Tyrconnel looked at him doubtfully. It was difficult to conceive a more dilapidated specimen of mankind even now. What he must have been in the past, it baffled the wit of man to conceive. The Archdeaconess, however, evidently thought a miracle had been worked.

" Perfectly wonderful! " she exclaimed, throwing up her hands.

" And you? Have you been here often? " asked he of the sorrowful countenance of Tyrconnel.

" This is my first time, and I hope it will be the last. My doctor thinks it will not be necessary for me to return," he rejoined.

The Colonel shook his head with sad foreboding.

" Once," he said, " is no use at all—you might just as well stop at home —I could tell you of many cases..." This he forthwith proceeded to do, with the most approved charnel-house details.

Tyrconnel turned away. This was hardly a cheerful conversation. Why is the path of virtue so hard and the other one so smooth? There was Coryton for instance, over the other side of the room apparently enjoying himself immensely with Sally, Pussie Prancewell, Gussie Gutter, and two or three men. Each of the three ladies carried a huge bouquet; they were chaffing and laughing to their hearts' content. Presently they all went off to the supper room together.

Tyrconnel felt quite sad. He wished the pretty golden-haired Fräulein, with whom he was so fond of sitting under the vine-clad arbour in the garden of the Hotel Dubigk, was here—she and her pretty sister. He had done his best to persuade them, but they would not come. 'Les Douleurs' society doesn't do such things,' they had told him, with an unconscious parody of Hedda Gabbler. But he really couldn't stand this woeful Colonel any longer. He was worse than old Wrigglesworth snarling in

yonder corner, or Lady Sumtyme Typsey and her
Backfisch daughter on the sofa at the top of the
room. So he took the Archdeaconess into the
supper-room and they had a bottle of sparkling
Moselle together.

There was a very uproarious party at the table
next them. Miss Popkins gave a comical sidelong
glance towards Tyrconnel as he came into the
room, and then seeing that he did not respond,
resumed her pleasing pastime of trying to teach a
little Spanish Count to speak English. Her method
was not that of Ollendorff, since it consisted chiefly
of making him repeat after her such brilliant
witticisms as 'Go, fry your face' and so forth, but
his attempt thereat seemed to provoke the party
to an altogether disproportionate amount of mirth.

Sally was looking very pretty this evening, all in
white, a symbol of her artless innocence. She
thought herself very much on the spot and so did
the Spanish Count, and he divided his attentions

equally between her and the mayonnaise. The rest of the party were all very lively; Miss Pussie Prancewell, late of the Gaiety, was repeating to the two young Englishmen from the Grand Monarque Hotel a private and unbowdlerized version of 'Helen of Troy,' a process which seemed to afford them an infinite amount of satisfaction.

Coryton was carrying on a brisk dialogue with Miss Gussie Gutter. That young woman was inclined to be quarrelsome at first, and made many scathing remarks when Sally sat down on her bouquet by mistake, but Coryton's tact had averted the threatened storm, and now under the genial influence of supper she waxed both generous and expansive. Gussie had a good heart with all her faults.

"What have you done with your—er—friend, Lord Welcher?" asked Coryton, as he plied her with more champagne. He wasn't paying for it, by the way. "Mr. Smith, you mean," corrected Gussie. "He went to his downey long ago. He

mustn't keep late hours while the cure's going on,
the doctor says, and as I'm over here to look after
him I see that the doctor's instructions are carried
out. 'What's the good of coming over here if you
don't, Johnnie?' I say. 'Right you are,' he says,
and turns in as meek as a lamb. No nonsense
with me, I can tell you—Poor old Johnnie! he's
a bad lot, I know, but I should be very sorry for
anything to happen to him all the same."

Here Gussie wiped away a furtive tear, but whether
born of Johnnie or of the champagne, who shall say?

"I daresay," she continued, with a sudden change
of tone, catching sight of the smile which played
for an instant about her listener's lips, "that you
think I only care for what I get out of him. But
I don't. It's rather the other way, I think; I pay
my way—look here." She whipped an envelope
out of her pocket and drew forth a cheque. "Do
you see what that is?—Forty quid; that is for one
week's work, four songs, or rather four times the

same song, at four different halls—the Tiv', the
Troc', the Pav' and the Oxford. I just hop into
a hansom and round I go—one after the other, and
the thing's done. £10 a week for each song. So
long as I can do that I have no need for anybody
to pay my bills," went on Gussie with dignity,
folding up the cheque again. "And the best of it
is," she added, dropping her voice confidentially,
"I can't sing a bit."

"Oh! don't say so!" put in Coryton affably.

"Not a bit," repeated Gussie, with engaging
frankness, "so don't come any of your blarney
over me. I often think of the man in the pit who
called out to me to 'Go 'ome and git your v'ice
sandpapered.' Great Scott! if I was to sandpaper
it, there wouldn't be any left. And you know it
too—but there—bless you, the public ain't musical—
they want to be amused, and I'm so 'sheek'."

"*Chic* indeed!" murmured Coryton as he filled
her glass again.

Miss Gutter quaffed it at a draught.

"Not bad tipple this," she said, "a trifle too sweet for my liking though." Then she gave Coryton a nudge, "Look at Sally there. How she's carrying on with that little Count! Did you *ever* see such a man? I wonder where he springs from! Shall we ask him?"

"It is wiser not to ask any questions at Les Douleurs," replied Coryton. "He may be a Prince in disguise; you know princes do come here in disguise occasionally."

"I know nothing about Princes," said Gussie, "I never knew one—I never got beyond a Duke. Hi—I say, Count where do you hail from?"

The Count knew that he was being addressed, but he didn't understand a word she was saying. So he removed his eyes from Sally and looked over the top of the trifle-dish at his interlocutor with a puzzled air.

"*Pardon?*" he asked tentatively.

"Tell him, Sally," said Miss Gutter, repeating her question. But Sally's knowledge of the German tongue did not run so far. So it had to be deputed to Wrigglesworth, one of Miss Prancewell's friends.

"He says that he comes from Spain where he has an ancient castle and huge estates—vast forests of cork trees, and acres of garlic," explained that worthy after he had translated the question.

"Tell that to the Marines," cried Gussie derisively, "I'm more than seven. Here! *Kellner*—waiter—whatever your name is, bring some more champagne—same as last.—Let us drink to the Count and his Castle in Spain. Tell the Count, Mr. Wriggles, what it's all about."

There was a fresh outburst of merriment round the table. When some people have advanced to a certain stage it takes but little to amuse them. Tyrconnel, sitting apart with respectability and the Archdeaconess, felt very much out of it. Yet surely it was not much to be 'out of'—this coarse revelry?

"Waiter," cried Gussie, "if you don't bring that fiz sharp, I'll say something that'll make your ears tingle. That's right, now fill up all of you. No heeltaps! Here's to our next merry meeting."

"I think," she said presently, "it's about time we were moving to the next room. I hear them striking up again. But I'm tired of slidin' and glidin' to those everlasting waltzes. It's time we had something more lively I say—they may be all right for these beer-swilling Germans, but I want to skip about a little.—Say, Sally—Pussie—shall we do the *pah de troy*, eh?"

But Miss Prancewell pleaded to be excused. She was here for her health, she said. Miss Popkins, however, was game.

"Oh! very well, we'll call it the *pah de doo* then!" continued Gussie, nothing daunted, "Sally and I will be able to manage it. My—won't the furriners stare. Come, Sally, are you ready? What are they playing now, a waltz or a polka?"

"I will go and see," said the astute Coryton, mindful of the bill. If he ate his supper with these sort of people, they must pay for the privilege. He wasn't going to do so.

In the doorway he came across Tyrconnel and the Archdeaconess and attached himself to them at once. Even Gussie would not dare to pursue him here. The sable skirts of the Archdeaconess were a sort of danger-signal to young persons of her type.

"If you knew how I have been wanting to come to you," murmured Coryton as they went back to the ball-room— "but it was so difficult to get away from those dreadful people."

"Dreadful indeed, Mr. Coryton," said the Archdeaconess severely, unfurling her fan. "I meant to have warned *you*. I have heard *all* about them—Goodness gracious!—what *are* they going to do now?"

Well might the Archdeaconess exclaim. Her virtuous eyes had never seen such a sight before. Gussie and Sally having kilted their skirts a little, started forth on their celebrated " *pah de doo* "—a dance chiefly remarkable for a sort of prancing step and a liberal display of ankle and frilling, something of the sort of dance young ladies now endeavour to imitate in London drawing-rooms before a select circle of bored acquaintances. They call it " skirt-dancing" and fondly imagine that it is so. But it isn't, unless it be skirt-dancing plus vulgarity and minus grace.

A waltz was being played when the two ladies first plunged into the throng, egged on by the plaudits of Miss Prancewell and her companions. Round and round the room they span, each round being wilder than before. If their object was, as Miss Gutter had put it, ' to make the furriners stare,' they certainly achieved it. Necks were craned forward, lorgnettes elevated, and exclamations of curiosity, wonder, surprise, amusement, admiration and disgust—the last chiefly from the matrons of the Anglo-American colony—were heard on every side. The English Chaplain withdrew his daughters from the scene, the Archdeaconess remonstrated, but the Master of the Ceremonies was at supper, and there was no one to interfere—even if there had been anything to interfere with. After all it was only two young ladies enjoying themselves after their own fashion.

"These English are so eccentric," said the Germans. And then at Les Douleurs one is used to strange sights.

The waltzers, becoming gradually aware that something unusual was going on in their midst, paused one by one, until at last Gussie and Sally were left in possession of the field. Stimulated by the sensation they were creating, possibly also by their libations of sparkling wine, they rose to the occasion and pranced more than ever. Round and

round, up and down, they flew, flushed, panting,
breathless—but undaunted. Sally lost her shoe,
but went on merrily just the same. Gussie's hair-
pins came out and her hair tumbled down her back
like a Mœnad's. At last the music closed with a
crash and they collapsed, exhausted, on a friendly
settee amid the enthusiastic plaudits of admiring
friends.

"Get me something to drink do, Count, if you
love me," gasped Sally. "My mouth's like a dust-
bin—Well, that *was* a dance, Gussie."

"Yes," panted that young lady, "we have given
them something to talk about at last—you bet.
Lend me some hair-pins do, Pussie, my hair's all
anyhow. Luckily it's my own."

"You should spare us a lock in honour of the
occasion," put in Wrigglesworth.

"Oh! you want a keep-sake do you?" exclaimed
Gussie. "Well, we can't part with our hair, can
we, Sally? But," stripping a ribbon from her dress

as she spoke, " we'll give you something else. Who wants one? "

The last impression the Archdeaconess had as she shook the dust off her feet and hurried from the room, was the picture of two Bacchanalian young women reclining on a couch, and giving away shreds of ribbon to the young men—and old men too—who crowded around them.

"Never," she said, as she descended the stairs, " have I-seen such a sight in Les Douleurs before; and never, I hope, shall I see it again."

CHAPTER III.

A COUNTRY HOUSE UP-TO-DATE.

'Shall I not take mine ease in mine inn?'
—Bacon, King Henry IV. Part I.

BLARNEY is built in a hollow, as all houses are
that date back beyond the modern craving for views.
Yet the prospect from the windows is by no means
an unpleasant one. They look along a kind of
valley, flanked by wooded ridges, which are the
boast of the whole country-side. The previous
owner, from stress of poverty, had made sad gaps
in the line of trees, and this gave the ridges a
somewhat toothless aspect. But the rich colouring

61

of the foliage, now in mid-autumn, with an occasional copper-beech standing out like a dagger-wound in the side of the forest still retained undeniable charms of its own.

Blarney has been associated in men's minds, ever since Elizabethan days, with the name of Tyrconnel. There was a Tyrconnel who was imprisoned for a conspiracy in favour of Mary, Queen of Scots, and lost sundry lands and manors, which were restored to another Tyrconnel, who fought with Drake and covered himself with wounds and honours in the process. There was a Tyrconnel who fought for King Charles, 'bidding the crop-headed parliament swing', and nearly losing Blarney in the process. There was a Tyrconnel at Sedgemoor and Killie-krankie, whose prowess lost him Wilton for a time, until the 'little gentleman in black velvet' did his good work and Anne Stuart gave back the stolen lands. There was a Tyrconnel with the Chevalier de Saint Georges in 1715, another at Fontenoy and

another at Gladsmuir, and one of them was created
Lord Baltinglass of Blarney by the Exile at Saint
Germains.   But they were younger sons, and the
head of the family, though he came within the
suspicions, was shrewd enough to escape the molesta-
tion of the ' wee, wee German Lairdies.'

Through all the troublous times of civil strife.
when loyalty was the most dangerous of disabilities,
this family of loyal gentlemen succeeded in maintaining, and not merely maintaining but also increasing the estate, through some erratic whim of
Fortune.   You may trace the stages of their
prosperity in the various additions and adornments
which the house underwent three or four times a
century.   They even survived the South Sea Bubble
and the rise of the Nabobs and the Revolution of
1832.

But the triumph of the Commercial System accomplished what neither foreign tyranny nor demol-
atry nor Billy Pitt's taxation had been able to do.

Railroads took away their peace of mind, Free Trade took away their income, and a succession of Reform Acts deprived them of their status in the country. The first steam whistle was the signal for the degeneracy of their race; the penny post and a cheap press relieved them of any wish to be anything but degenerate; labourers became members of parliament and the Tyrconnels ceased to take any interest in anything that might further happen to the country.

An ancient and glorious house, whose traditions of stainless loyalty and honour remained almost their only heritage, succumbed before the Spirit of the Age. Fortune, love of country, desire for perpetuation died away in the house of Tyrconnel; and all its noble memories centred in the person of one woman, a distant cousin of the last heir of Blarney.

She was insignificant of stature and unprepossessing of appearance, but her nose had the true

Tyrconnel arch and she possessed all the true Tyrconnel charm of manner. She seemed to have resuscitated in her character all the ambition of the race of soldiers from which she sprang. But their pride and their prejudices had not descended upon the heiress and her ambition prompted her to make submission to the Spirit of the Age. She did so by marrying a millionaire soap-boiler, named Simpson, and making him take her name as well as her impoverished estates. So great was her astuteness, that she actually succeeded in obtaining the revival of the old title of Baltinglass of Blarney, before she died of consumption a few years after giving birth to Wilfrid Tyrconnel.

It was a triumph which did her head credit, if not her heart, and Wilfrid, when he thought it over, admitted that Blarney might have passed to less worthy hands.

The first impression of Blarney, as you approach

it through the park, is of size. It is a long, low, straggling house of red brick, constantly added to at various epochs in its three century existence, and presents—with its conservatories, its library and billiard-room, each approached by long galleries, its stables, outhouses, and observatory—the appearance of a village rather than a house.

This was what struck a waggonetteful of people now on their way to Blarney as the guests for the first time of Lord Baltinglass. They included Sir Cincinnatus Spreadeagle, M.P., a professional politician of alien origin, who had lately been rewarded for a course of spreadeagle speeches in the provinces and a golden silence in the House with a knighthood instead of the baronetcy he had asked for; Lady Giddy and her brother, Colonel Lockhart; Mr. Rupert Clifford of the White Rose Society; Miss Mudlark, a Canadian girl, whose acquaintance Miss Tyrconnel had made in the reading-room of the Grosvenor Hotel; her friend,

Miss Connecticut of New York; and Mr. Alfred Seemann, late M.P. for Penge.

The drive had been a rather merry one, Lady Giddy making great fun of Sir Cincinnatus in a quiet way, which led that orator to think he was being flirted with and nearly sent everybody else into convulsions of laughter; the transatlantic young ladies giving their impressions of English society with the approved transatlantic freedom and forced originality; and Colonel Lockhart entertaining all who could be prevailed upon to listen with startling stories of his prowess with rod and gun. He had a trick, while describing his phenomenal shots, of putting up his arms in the attitude of firing, which gave the stories a certain dramatic point, but he showed signs of getting huffy when, after a story that required more gesticulation than usual, Seemann asked him quietly, "Did you ever shoot with the long bow, old man?"

As the house appeared in sight, they fell to discuss-

ing their host and the manner of hospitality that
awaited them. "I am told it is like staying at
an hotel,"said Clifford, in his drawling voice. "No
one troubles to entertain you, but you can be
tolerably comfortable if you bribe and bully the
servants sufficiently."

"That's what I like," said Seemann, beaming
through his spectacles. "My ideal host is a vulgar
beast, who slaps you on the shoulders and tells
you his house is 'Liberty 'All.' Nothing is so
disagreeable as having your day mapped out for
you by someone who does not understand your
habits."

"Well, so long as one doesn't stay here a Sunday,
I imagine it's all right," said Lady Giddy. "You
know Miss Tyrconnel is a Presbyterian or a Shaker
or some such thing and she turns the house into
a sort of quarantine,—to fumigate one's sins of the
week, I suppose. Poor Maria Miles spent a Sunday
here once upon a time and can tell you blood-

curdling tales about it. Cold meals! Three times
to church! No amusements of any sort or kind,
not even a walk in the garden, and family prayers
at night with readings from Evangelical divines,—
you know the kind of thing I mean."

"I am thankful to say I don't," said Sir Cincinnatus Spreadeagle ogling Lady Giddy with a bilious
eye.

"What! Not when you stay with Lady Cocka-
doodledoo?" Lady Giddy asked sarcastically.

"I never do," he replied sulkily.

"I guess I'd hate that, wouldn't you, Kit?"
said Miss Connecticut to Miss Mudlark. "We'd have
to go upstairs with yellow-backs and cigarettes."

Miss Mudlark put her thumb in her mouth and
simpered in a silly way, which she imagined to be
suggestive of youth and innocence.

"Miss Simpson would soon rout you out if you
did," said Lady Giddy in the abrupt manner she
always assumed towards her own sex.

"My dear Gerty," whispered Colonel Lockhart, as they now drove up to the front door, "you really must be careful not to call the old woman Simpson. She changed her name to Tyrconnel when her brother got his peerage, and is frightfully touchy about it."

"Oh! But I am a privileged person about names. Why, even Mr. Seemann forgives me when I pronounce his in the English way," she added laughing, as they entered the house, "instead of 'Zay-man,' which he clings to for some unknown reason."

They found Miss Tyrconnel alone in the drawing-room, sitting upright in a hard-backed chair with a large family Bible open upon her knees at the second epistle of Paul the Apostle to the Corinthians. As the guests came in, she took off her gold spectacles and wiped them very deliberately; placed a big red book-marker, with 'Their worm dieth not' elaborately embroidered upon it, between the pages where she had just left off reading; and laid the volume reverently on a music-stool beside her, so that the words 'Holy Bible' might be conspicuously visible to everyone.

By this time the whole party had come into the room and was standing grouped around the hostess, waiting until the termination of these devotions allowed her to greet them. This at length she did, in a stiff way intended to convey an impression both of piety and dignity.

"Will you be seated?" she asked condescendingly. "Oh, not there, I pray you," she added hastily, as Sir Cincinnatus Spreadeagle was settling his portly person upon the music stool and its precious burden.

"All right, thanks," replied the culprit heartily, "I'll move this book, if you'll allow me," and he proceeded to place it carelessly on the top of a pile of light operatic music, with which Violet Tresillian had been beguiling the morning hours.

Miss Tyrconnel frowned, rose slowly, took up the Bible in an ostentatious manner, the corners of her mouth drooping austerely as she did so, and stowed it away in a large ormolu cupboard near the door. Meanwhile Sir Cincinnatus, rather red in the face, was trying to pass off the incident by winking at Lady Giddy, but she, enjoying his embarrassment, looked at him as if he had been guilty of some very grave solecism and the others took their cue from her.

"You have put your foot in it this time," Seemann whispered in his ear. "I shouldn't wonder if she told you to leave the house to-morrow morning."

Now it would not at all have suited Sir Cincinnatus' arrangements to leave the house next morning, and his jaw fell at the suggestion. But Miss Tyrconnel showed no trace of resentment and was returning to her seat with all the airs and graces of a martyr about to offer the other cheek to the smiter. She sat down again angularly, like a soldier shouldering arms, and then, folding her hands religiously in her lap, said, "I daresay you would like some tea."

Everybody's face brightened, for it was a quarter past four and it had been necessary to lunch very early. The faces soon fell again, however, as she added, "Our tea-time is five o'clock," as if it were a feast immutable according to the law of the Medes and Persians.

There was a solemn, hungry pause, during which Miss Mudlark vainly tried to put up Miss Connecticut to ask for whiskies and sodas. Then Miss Tyrconnel said to the ladies, "Perhaps you would like to see your rooms," and ushered them out of the door.

"This is cheerful," said Sir Cincinnatus gloomily. "I think I shall go and see if I haven't got a flask and some biscuits in my dressing-bag."

Just then the sound of much laughter fell agreeably on their jaded ears and there burst in from the conservatory Violet Tresillian, Pimlico, Gaverigan, Coryton, Williams and Wilmot, all in the highest spirits after the tedium of a game of golf. The son of the house had gone to the station to meet Mrs. Miles and Gwendolen, who were arriving that afternoon by a later train.

" What are you fellows looking so gloomy about ? " asked Gaverigan, after greetings had been exchanged.

" We're ravenously hungry and thirsty and we've just been told we can't have anything for three quarters of an hour," said Sir Cincinnatus dolefully.

" Ha ! ha ! That's easily remedied," laughed Gaverigan, ringing the bell. " You don't know the ways of the house yet. Miss Tyrconnel's a very worthy woman, but no one takes very much notice of her here. She is hostess only by courtesy title. Give it a name, that's all. George," (this to the footman) " take something to drink into the hall."

" I didn't know you were to be our host, Harold,"

said Colonel Lockhart, laughing at the coolness of
the order.

"Gaverigan's a host in himself," said Seemann,
whose spirits were rapidly reviving at the prospect
of refreshment.

" Well, really, Mr. Clifford," said Miss Connecticut, who had just slipped back from being shown
her room, "I guessed you were just joking when
you said it was like staying at an hotel here, but
I found my room numbered just like the Metropole,
and a notice stuck up over my bed saying that
'All luggage must be ready 15 minutes before the
departure of the train' and another to say 'No
reading in bed.' And this looks like it too, calling
for drinks all round on your own hook. Do you
all do that or is it just one of Mr. Gaverigan's
bluffs?"

" We all do it when we have a mind to," said
Coryton in confidential tones, as if imparting a
cabinet secret; "for my part, I infinitely prefer it

to an hotel. You get better attendance and more comforts, with the additional advantage that you have no reckoning to pay when you leave. I saw an advertisement the other day of a place at the sea-side that called itself 'A home away from home,' and it struck me that was a good name for this one. You have all the advantage of being away from home as well as that of being able to make yourself entirely at home. I think I shall suggest to Lord Baltinglass that he should advertise the place under that name."

"I quite agree with you," said Gaverigan joining in rather superciliously. "I can't make out why everybody doesn't come and stay here. I hate country houses as a rule because you are expected either to amuse people or be amused yourself, and I don't know which is the worse."

Further comment was cut short by a migration to the hall, where there was a simultaneous entrance of refreshments by one door and of Lord Baltinglass

with Lord Southwark by the other. The host,
although of the lowest origin and having no
pretentions to breeding, had yet brushed sufficiently
with society to pick up something of the off-hand
manners, which are supposed to denote smartness
but really only connote impertinence. So he only
greeted the new arrivals with a toss of the head
and a careless shake of the hand and led his
companion to a little inner room, furnished in the
Turkish fashion, with luxurious divans and glittering
embroidered cushions, where the very atmosphere
seemed suggestive of Oriental intrigues and privy
conspiracy.

" Which is our host? " whispered Miss Connecticut
in Miss Mudlark's ear as they passed. " The little
sleek man, I guess, with the bone studs and cardboard
tie. If I hadn't known he was a real lord, I'd
have told him to bring me some ice-water."

" Hush! That's the Marquis of Southwark, a
Cabinet Minister, with a pedigree that reaches back

to the ancient Britons. You know they used to stain their bodies with woad; that's the reason his blood's so blue. The fat man, with the silky beard and the nose like a yam, is Baltinglass, the Soap-King. But I say, here's drinks at last. Come along and see a man."

CHAPTER IV.

IN THE CONSERVATORY.

Marriage is like a beleaguered fortress: those
who are outside wish to enter, while those
who are inside want to get out.
—ARAB PROVERB.

THE hall was the favourite resort at Blarney.
It was a sort of tea-room, smoking-room, cloak-
room, boudoir and general lounge all in one, and
visitors were agreed that it was far and away the
most comfortable room in the house. It was over-
furnished, of course; every room was over-furnished
there. But the furniture aimed a little more at
comfort than it did in the other rooms, though it

was still comfort tempered by display. There were too many coats of mail on the walls, and the best and softest seat near the great open fire-place exposed you to banging your head against a halle-barde if you did not sit down with circumspection. Even then you did not escape from the all-pervading coronets, which, indeed, it was impossible to escape from anywhere at Blarney. There were coronets in bas-relief on the chairs, coronets embroidered on the cushions, coronets in haut-relief on the carved chimney, coronets on the fire-screen, even a coronet in the pattern of the Oriental rugs and coronets among the shadows cast by the fire-logs.

"Our host is, at any rate, determined," said Clifford contemptuously, " that we shall not forget the respect due to his title. I wonder he doesn't wear his coronet at dinner, as English peers are generally supposed to do by the American colonists."

You did not escape from the coronets, but they were less irritating when you had a comfortable chair and could close your eyes to them than they were, say, in the drawing-room, among the gilt spindle-legged chairs and the ormolu cabinets.

If Blarney was a village, this was the village club. Everybody came here when he was in a gossiping mood or wanted refreshments; letters and newspapers were always exposed here; conspiracies hatched; characters dissected; the opposite sex discussed and travestied; and both sexes married and given in marriage by kind observers in the most grotesque and unsuitable manner imaginable.

While the corks were popping in the hall, the two peers were deep in discussion about the apportionment of certain 'safe seats,' over which their control was in reality not quite so complete as they imagined.

" I suppose you'll want the Bantam Division of Hodgeshire for that boy of yours, Baltinglass," said Lord Southwark, lighting a cigarette, and leaning the back of his head against the chimney-piece.

" Well, I make no objection, but I shall count on your support in West Southwark for some plans of my own. If we are to do anything in either of those places, we must agree to pull together."

" Quite so," returned the other, who had not changed his manner of speech since he boiled soap, " but I'd like to 'ear what your plans are."

" Lord Pimlico is to have the seat eventually, as you are doubtless aware," began Lord Southwark stiffly. "Eventually," he repeated, as the other gave a contemptuous grunt. " I am quite aware that he is not ready to enter Parliament yet. I see nothing to smile at in what I am saying. He does not himself wish it. But in a few years, when he has sown his wild oats, he will do it to please me. The thing is expected, and I shall make a point of it with him."

" And in the meantime?"

" In the meantime, I must find some warming-pan or other. Wrigglesworth is positive that since

Mr. Loose-Fyshe put pepper into a cream-tart, the Pharisees of Southwark won't support him and, unless he retires (which he refuses to do) it will simply be a walk over for the Conservative nominee. If I had a good private secretary, whom I could trust, he should have the seat for the next three or four years. But I am in despair about private secretaries. They are all either sharps or flats and I am rapidly coming to the conclusion that one has less trouble in the long run by being one's own private secretary."

" I can recommend you a capital fellow. He's a most high-principled young man and as clever as they make 'em. A son of that old fox, Spencer Coryton, who was Judge-Advocate General in one of Disraeli's administrations."

"I remember him,—one of those professional, ministers who have done so much to degrade political life. A useful varlet, but not to be trusted round the corner."

"Well, you can trust the boy. He's as good as gold. I don't mind admitting to you that I am under some obligations to him and I'd go a good bit out of my way to do him a good turn. If you'd make him your secretary and put him in for West Southwark, you'd not regret it, I'll warrant ye."

"I will think your suggestion over and speak with you again upon it. I saw the youth once at Cambridge and was favourably impressed. I suppose he would not exact a heavy salary, eh? I am not a believer in over-paying people."

"He must have a certain income of his own, but you'll find him well worth all you like to give him. I'm not one that throws good money away, as you may imagine, but whenever I've given him a cheque for a hundred or so, I've found him fairly earn it."

Meanwhile, the subject of this dialogue was occupied with very different considerations. Coryton and Violet were in the billiard-room, organizing a kind of extempore theatricals which Lady Giddy had proposed and everyone carried by acclamation.

"It's a sort of Dumb Crambo, if you know what that means," Violet was explaining to Miss Connecticut, "only it isn't dumb. We invent our dialogues as we go along. First, we choose a word. Then we choose words beginning with each of its letters and act them one after the other. Then we act the word itself, and the audience has to guess it."

" I always find in these sort of entertainments, the great difficulty is to get an audience," said Mr. Seemann garrulously. "People are ready to take any part you like to offer them, except that one. That's where I come in. I ask nothing better than to be allowed to play audience."

"Yes, you'll do very well," Violet rattled on. "Now, are you quite sure you all understand?"

"No, I am afraid it's a little beyond me," put in Miss Mudlark, who felt she had not received sufficient attention during the last ten minutes.

"You tiresome child. I'll take a word as an example. Suppose we say Noah."

"Let me see. He was the man who found Joseph among the bulrushes, wasn't he?"

"See here, Kit, you just be careful," said Miss Connecticut, shaking a warning finger at her friend. "If Miss Tyrconnel heard you, she'd pretty well pull the house down about your ears."

"Do you never play with Noah's Arks in the wilds of Canada?" asked Violet contemptuously. "Now let me see. N, O, A, H. N might be Nebuchadnezzar eating grass. That's rather an effective scene. We had it at Caradoc Castle last year. O might be Titus Oates in the pillory. A Anthony and Cleopatra,—with Miss Haviland as Cleopatra," she added mischievously. "Then H— Henry the Eighth,—Pim is admirably cut out for that part. Last of all, the word itself, Noah, with animals and rainbows and all that kind of game."

"And here's the very man to play the leading

part," exclaimed Lady Giddy, clapping her hands, as Sir Cincinnatus Spreadeagle entered the room. "Don't you think he'd make an admirable Noah after dinner with a bottle of port under each arm and two more inside him?"

Further consultations were interrupted by the dressing-bell and in five minutes everybody had gone upstairs. Violet and Coryton were the last to leave. Just as she was skipping off after the little Yankee, he put his hand on her arm and said with unusual tenderness, " Vixie, please arrange for us to have a quiet chat before we leave Blarney. I have got no end to say to you and it's so hard to get a moment alone with you in this rabble."

Violet looked up at him quickly with a half grateful expression in her eyes.

" All right," she said, checking the sentimental mood, which had begun to steal over her, " we'll get Gwen to sing after dinner, and then slink out and spoon in the conservatory. D'you know, Poley,

old boy, I like you better than any of them. I wish
you had ten thousand a year. 'Pon my word I do."

" As long as we have enough for our modest wants,"
he returned half-ironically, " why sigh for more? "

" Yes, but our wants ain't modest, that's what
plays the deuce with us," she laughed.

" I don't know. A little box of a house in Mayfair,
a good cook, a smart brougham and a long-suffering
set of tradesmen. We could do that on two or
three thousand a year."

Violet's face lighted up. Well, if he had got
that, it might really be worth while. They would
certainly get on very well together and Coryton
was a man who might easily 'arrive' some day,
as they say over the water. Meanwhile, she hated
having to dress in a hurry and it was getting
late. So she waved her hand airily at him and flew
up the broad stairs three and four at a time.

When she came down, she was evidently well
satisfied with the prowess of her maid and peacocked

into the room with all the self-confidence engendered
by a perfectly fitting dress perfectly put on. It
was made of pale rose-pink crêpe-de-Chine, picked
up at a sale at Liberty's. The skirt was very full
and fluffy, caught up here and there by bunches of
pearls,—not ropes of pearls. like Disraeli's heroines,
but little strings of them, at three and elevenpence
the yard. Her baby-bodice, perhaps cut a little
too low, was drawn in by a wide stay embroidered
with pearls. It was a triumph of art over impe-
cuniosity and, except to a very well initiated observer,
conveyed an impression of unstinted dress-makers.
No one would have guessed that it was all the
work of the little French dress-maker, whom she
had pulled out of a ticklish scrape at Trouville one
summer and taken on as her maid and devoted
worshipper at twenty pounds a year.

Violet's figure was now well developed; she had
a long wasp-like waist and, as she came smiling
into the room, Wilmot, who had met some of the

Paris painter-men and consequently liked to air his knowledge of art, whispered in Williams's ear that she reminded him of a van Beers's girl in a Christmas number. Williams, who had not been to Paris, would have it that she was more like a creation of Sir Frederick Leighton and pointed conclusively to the pink velvet bands that restrained the wealth of golden hair, apparently threatening to burst out as from a horn of plenty.

Violet's hair was the best among her 'points', as Pim and his cousin Theodora Gargoyle said when they discussed her, and Julie, her maid, certainly knew how to make the most of it, as she did of everything about her mistress.

When Violet came into the drawing-room, she found an unusual commotion going on. It was all owing to Miss Tyrconnel, who, by way of marking her resentment at the number of strange guests invited to the house, had announced that she hadn't the ghost of an idea how she was to send them all in to dinner. Lady Giddy precipitated herself upon the opportunity: let Miss Tyrconnel leave everything to her and it should all be done most admirably. Miss Tyrconnel did not quite like the idea, but, like most self-made people, she had a lurking sense of respect for her social superiors and besides, after her incautious avowal, it was not easy to back out of the offer. So Lady Giddy announced to all and sundry that, instead of going into dinner in the usual orthodox way, they were to go in by lot. It was quite the latest *chic*, she assured Lord Baltinglass, who seemed rather doubtful about it. The Broadakers always did it when they had a big house party and Prince Pumpenheim had thought it very funny during his last visit to England.

This had silenced the host's last scruple and here were two hats on the table full of little folded bits of paper. One contained the names of various historical or mythological male characters and the

other those of the corresponding female ones. All
the men had to draw from one hat and all the
ladies from the other; then they found themselves
more or less grotesquely paired off.

Screams of laughter greeted the announcement
of each fresh draw, culminating in unending merriment when Sir Cincinnatus Spreadeagle was drawn
as Romeo to Miss Tyrconnel's Juliet. Lord
Baltinglass smiled grimly when he found himself
allotted the character of Adam to Mrs. de Courcy
Miles's Eve, asking—to Miss Tyrconnel's grave
concern,—whether the part was to be played in
costume. Everyone agreed that Mr. Rupert Clifford
and Lady Elizabeth Gargoyle, a stout lady with
Titian-like hair, were hardly used in being sent
in as Jumbo and Alice, for their worst enemies
could not accuse them of excessive *embonpoint;* but
Coryton and Violet as Faust and Marguerite met
with general approval, as did Wilfrid Tyrconnel
and Gwendolen Haviland in the *rôle* of Darby and

Joan. Miss Mauresk and Colonel Lockhart were
Venus and Adonis, the latter a somewhat juvenile
part for the superannuated beau. Sir Edward
Tresillian thought the game rather funny until he
drew Punch to Miss Connecticut's Judy. Mr.
Seemann was no less ridiculous, though he thought
himself more fortunate, as Anthony with Miss
Mudlark for an incongruous Cleopatra. Pimlico
and Miss Theodora Gargoyle were the Bulbul and
the Rose; Cupid and Psyche were represented:
Cupid by a little shrivelled up old man in a fez,
who turned out to be the Turkish ambassador, and
Psyche by the 'Archdeaconess,' who had been asked
by Miss Tyrconnel as a return for her kindness to
Wilfrid at Les Douleurs; Gaverigan and Lady
Giddy were Fox and Goose; Lord Southwark and
Lady Vieille were the Mouse and the Lion, or
Lion-hunter, as Lady Giddy said it ought to be.
Owing to a dearth of ladies there were two extra
men's tickets, which appropriately enough, sent

in Williams and Wilmot as David and Jonathan.

When the various characters at last made their
way into the dining-room, they found cards on the
plates with their new names; Jumbo and Joan
were next each other, while the Fox was in
dangerous proximity to the Bulbul. Adam and
Eve were subjected to great chaff when apple-
tart came round. Altogether the pastime afforded
an agreeable diversion, but Miss Tyrconnel registered a
mental vow that she would never tolerate such foolery
again, and when, later on, Lady Giddy proposed a
game of hide-and-seek in the garden by moonlight,
she entered an abrupt and disconcerting negative.

Coryton and Violet were, however, able to
arrange a small variation of that game for themselves
after dinner on a cosy settee behind a big palm
in the conservatory.

"Well, Poley, my charming Faust-up-to-date,
what have you to tell your Marguerite?" she asked
playfully, when they were settled.

" Something she knows very well already," he replied, taking up her chubby little hand in his and looking intently at it, half sentimentally, half wonderingly.

" Yes, but is it prudent?" she said thoughtfully, looking out into the moonbeams, which danced in the splashing fountain just outside. " We are very good friends and should probably remain so. That is the best safeguard for a happy marriage. It can give melodramatic love a stone and a beating, as Theodora would say. But couldn't we both do a great deal better for ourselves elsewhere? Wouldn't it be criminally idiotic not to marry for tin ?"

" No. That is the mistake made by what are called 'fly jugginses'. The world is not divided into two broad divisions, sharpers and jays. There are all sorts of gradations between them. Perhaps the commonest is the juggins by nature, who has been sufficiently emancipated to fancy himself 'fly'.

The 'fly juggins' is a far commoner type than people suppose. The three-card-trick is directed solely against him. He is shown the corner turned down and fancies he is going to cheat the three-card-trick man, with the result that he only gets cheated himself. Astuteness is all very well, but it is not elastic beyond a certain point and may be overdone."

" Yes, I remember hearing about your brush with sharpers on the way to Newmarket, but I don't think you came second best out of that encounter. However, come back to your muttons, meaning me."

"I was only going to say, that people who marry for money only, are 'fly jugginses,' who overreach themselves. After all, we should be comfortably off, as I was saying before dinner, and I don't see what more we should need. You've got money, or will have, and I have a certain amount. We shan't starve or be restricted to three-course dinners, or driven to live in a flat at Putney!"

"No, I am sure we should have a very good time as long as things went smoothly. But what do you propose? Not that we should place ourselves in the ridiculous position of telling the world we are engaged?"

"Would that be so very ridiculous?" asked Coryton, rather hurt.

"I don't suppose *we* should be ridiculous. But most people are when they're engaged. I almost think I should feel shy, though I never have yet. If we are to be engaged, let's only announce it about a day before the wedding."

"Then we'd get no presents."

"Well, a week."

"All right. But between ourselves it's an engagement all the same, isn't it, Vixie? Just give me one little kiss to seal the bargain."

Violet gave a slight blush, an unheard-of thing

for her. She had kissed many young men before now among her acquaintances, but somehow this seemed different. However, after a slight show of hesitation, she put up her cherry lips, with her eyes sparkling in quite an unnatural way, and there was a sort of tremble in her eyelashes as she looked up at him.

Just at this psychological moment, however, the spell was rudely broken by the appearance of Mrs. de Courcy Miles, who had heard many inquiries for Violet to play the game they arranged before dinner, and had good-naturedly volunteered to find her. Violet, for once taken off her guard, answered her rudely, with some display of impatience.

"Can't you see that I'm busy?" she remonstrated. " Why can't you mind your own concerns and leave me alone, instead of bursting in like a hurricane just when I was cosy and amused? You quite startled me."

"So I perceive," said Mrs. Miles drily, as she turned upon her heel.

When she was gone, the spirit of their dream was altered and neither proposed to recommence the interrupted kiss. They said nothing for a while, but sat staring moodily at the tips of their toes. At last Violet said in a constrained way, " Let's go to the drawing-room," and they stepped blinkingly into the over-lighted house.

CHAPTER V.

THE MELTING OF THE ICE-MAIDEN.

Hide, O, hide those hills of snow,
   Which thy frozen bosom bears,
On whose tops the pinks that grow
   Are of those that April wears!
But first set my poor heart free,
Bound in those icy chains by thee.
           —BEAUMONT AND FLETCHER.

Virtue. like an ice-berg, chills most when
   it thaws.   —PICHEGRU.

GWENDOLEN now met Wilfrid for the first time since his abrupt departure from Cambridge seven months before. She had made a great show of reluctance about accepting Lord Baltinglass's invitation to

100

Blarney, much to Mrs. de Courcy Miles's amazement and disgust. But in her heart of hearts the girl knew that she would yield. She had not known how dear Tyrconnel was to her until they were parted, apparently for ever.

She had the bump of veneration very strongly developed, and numbered respect for the powers that be, such as college authorities, among the highest duties. Like all those who have not yet tasted the fruit of the tree of good and evil, she was utterly intolerant of the smallest wandering from the path of duty and would admit no distinction between the most heinous moral offences and the most trivial peccadilloes. One of her favourite phrases was, that there are no such things as little sins.

There was also a certain amount of injured pride in her resentment against Wilfrid Tyrconnel. She had not exactly mapped out for herself the *rôle* of the beautiful saint marrying and reclaiming the dissolute rake, but her schemes were leavened by some such idea. He was weak, but well meaning; she was a Christian woman. Was he not to be snatched as a brand from the burning and by her intervention? Was she not to be the humble instrument of rescuing him for the church of Christ and guarding his goings so that his footsteps slipped not? She had been so happy in that thought, so proud of her first success as an evangelist, and at the very first trial all her hopes, all her calculations, all her triumphs had come to an abrupt end like a child's house of cards.

In her moments of austerest self-communing, she attributed the failure to her pride and thanked Heaven for the timely lesson. But even then she was still woman enough to feel that the fault of her failure was Tyrconnel's and to cherish a grievance against him for her disappointment. He had been in such a hurry to forsake the narrow path, almost before the vows were silent upon his lips.

How little in earnest he must have been, how idle must have been his promises of amendment, his dedication of himself to the service of God! And if so, how idle too, perhaps, his passionate protestations of love for her. She had said she would trust him and he had been so hasty to prove to her that he was utterly untrustworthy. All this and more she had written in her precise style to him while he was at Les Douleurs. Pages and pages of remonstrance, and reflection, and lamentation on that horrid 'foreign' writing-paper, where all the ink shows through.

"Good Heavens!" Tyrconnel had thought to himself, in the intervals between his moods of infatuation and penitence, "if she makes such an outcry over my being sent down from Cambridge for keeping late hours, what would she not say if she knew of my acquaintance with Sally Popkins or even of my passion for gambling?"

He reflected bitterly that it was always so with

religious people: the gospel of forgiveness was a favourite theory with them, but most uncongenial in practice.

Gwendolen only required a certain amount of pressing to take her to Blarney. Coryton had told Wilfrid at Les Douleurs that Mrs. de Courcy Miles might be trusted to see to that, but Mrs de Courcy Miles, with all her boasted social astuteness, was painfully destitute of tact in dealing with such a girl as Gwendolen and her dogmatic methods of argument had often had the effect of confirming the girl in her rebellions. It was perhaps the strongest proof of Gwendolen's real wish to come to Blarney, that she consented to do so in spite of her aunt's ill-judged nagging.

Anyhow, here was Gwendolen at Blarney after all. It was not until she was actually on her way there that she fully realized what a concession she was making. By all rights, he should have come to her and abased himself before her, like the

prodigal that he was, and implored her to be gra-
ciously pleased to accord her forgiveness. And that
forgiveness she would not have required very, very
long persuasion to induce her to concede. Her
pride rebelled again at the idea of coming thus to
his house, as *his* guest, in obedience to *his* command, at the very first beck. And yet there
remained in her a sufficiency of sex to make her
heart confess that, in spite of all, she was glad to
have consented. Do what she would, her heart
leaped joyously within her at the prospect of seeing
'her boy' once more.

Their first meeting was somewhat constrained,
for he had missed her at the station after all and,
as a number of people were present, it was impossible to make much display of emotion.

"I hear you have become quite a traveller, Wilfrid," Mrs. de Courcy Miles exclaimed with a show
of heartiness. "Gwen and I have been looking
forward so much to getting you to give us all your

experiences. Can't say the German waters have agreed with you, though," she added, imagining she was displaying a tender solicitude. "You'll have to take to cub-hunting or something to get you back your colour."

"How d'you do, Wilfrid?"

"Why, Gwen!"

That was all, but their eyes lighted up as they shook hands and Lady Giddy whispered to Violet that she believed there must be something in it after all.

Violet smiled. "Poor old Pigeon!" was all she said.

During dinner the conversation had been boisterous and general. Tyrconnel tried to engage Gwendolen upon such a safe topic as a recent discovery of pottery in the neighbourhood, but she answered in a way that, without actually conveying a snub, made it almost impossible to follow up the subject. Moreover, she seemed to prefer to discuss Jacobitism with her other neighbour, Rupert Clifford, and to enter upon a dogmatic eulogy of Hampden, which sadly disconcerted that very polite gentleman.

It was not until some time after dinner, just when that little scene was being enacted between Coryton and Violet in the conservatory, that she found the opportunity she had been seeking of having private speech with Wilfrid in one of the many nooks for which Blarney was famous.

"You may have thought me rude," she said, settling herself in a window seat of the library and making room for him by her side, "but I couldn't 'make talk' with you at dinner on all sorts of trivial subjects, when my heart was full and sad."

"Sad! Gwendolen," he whispered reproachfully; "I hoped that you were happy to see me again, after all these ages. I thought you would be content to let bygones be bygones."

"Ah! Wilfrid, bygones never can be completely bygones. One may forgive, but one cannot so easily forget. The wounds of the heart are far more serious and slow to heal than those of the body. I am of a different temperament to you. I believe you suffer acutely and then shake your suffering off, never to think of it again. That I cannot do. What I have suffered all these months you can never know. If I live to be a hundred, I shall never forget the shame of it all."

" The shame!"

" Yes, the shame. We were to be all in all to each other, to fight the good fight side by side. You had promised me to turn over a new leaf, yet scarcely were you out of my sight than I heard of your backsliding. Some dreadful orgy far into the night, bringing you into conflict with the authorities and compelling them to expel you from the University. The details of that affair I have never sought to know. The shame of it was enough for me. As we then stood to one another, your shame was my shame."

"Don't be too hard upon me for the folly of an unguarded hour."

"Do not talk to me of an 'unguarded hour.' I have no patience with such nonsense. You forget the pain to me of having so misplaced my confidence. I thought I could trust you, Wilfrid. It was hard,—very, very hard,—to find how unworthy you were of being loved."

"Oh! Gwen," was all he could say, in a low, choked voice.

"Yes, Wilfrid," she replied, looking him full in the face with her big, mournful guardian angel's eyes. "It has been a sad, sad time. It hurts me even now to think of it. I am ready to believe that all this has been a lesson to you, I will try to believe that you are going to turn over a new leaf. But the old trust is dead and cannot be brought back to life and, without that trust, there can be no such thing as perfect love. Until you have given practical proof of your repentance, how can you expect me to believe in you? It is heart-breaking to me to have to speak to you like this, but what else can I say?"

" Say that you forgive me."

" It is not of me that you must ask forgiveness. There is only One Who can forgive sins."

And she turned up the whites of her big eyes.

" Give me a chance, Gwen," he pleaded humbly. " I have had a lesson which has made an altered man of me. Let us forget all about it."

" That can scarcely be."

And she pressed her beautiful lips austerely together.

" But you do not throw me over entirely. It is not all at an end between us. Only tell me there is still hope for me."

" There is always hope. Hope remains long after all else is lost."

" You will marry me some day, if—if you find that you can believe in me again," he pleaded with gathering joy, as he read the light of love beaming on him from her bright eyes.

" That is for the future to decide," she replied in softer tones than she had yet used.

The hum of the guests in the drawing-room sounded very far off. There was a solemn hush in the lofty room with its wilderness of books; only the wood-fire crackled cheerfully in the big old-fashioned grate and set bogey-like shadows dancing in the corners of the room. The two reading-lamps, with their scarlet shades, gave out a dim rosiness, which transfigured—as limelight trans-figures—the calm,. holy expression of the ice-maiden. It was the very scene, with all appropriate surroundings, for a declaration. Soft music was alone required to make it theatrically complete. The sensation of this came over them both suddenly and they looked into each others eyes with all the old tenderness. A blush spread over Gwendolen's face, giving it another and a deeper coating of colour to that which she owed to the scarlet lamp-shades. His hand stole into hers and she made an instinctive movement as if to withdraw it, then changed her mind and let it rest in his. He bent down and reverently imprinted a kiss on her long, white fingers.

"I love you, Wilfrid," she said with infinite tenderness. "I love you very, very dearly. I only wish you to be true to yourself. I pray night and morning and shall pray so long as I have breath that you may have grace to withstand temptation."

"Hullo, there you are," Lord Pimlico's hearty voice broke startlingly upon their ears as they came out into the corridor. "We've been looking for you everywhere. They're gettin' up a game of cutlets. Rippin' fun. Come along. The arch-deaconess began the game on old Spreadeagle's knees and has been exacting the funniest forfeits from that stupid little Seemann."

And he hurried on after his cousin, Theodora Gargoyle, who had a little more sense of the fitness of things than he and preferred not to wait Gwendolen's answer.

"Yes, come along," said Violet, who had come up just then, on her way from the conservatory with Coryton. "We needn't join in Pim's mad games and one can always talk best in a rowdy crowd."

"Have you just come into a fortune, Pidge, old chap?" asked Coryton with a cold malevolent gleam in his eyes, that belied the geniality of his words. He took Tyrconnel's arm and they fell into line behind the girls, who were turning their steps towards the drawing-room.

"Fortune seems at last to be turning her nose my way," replied Tyrconnel, blushing violently. "I mustn't say too much. But—but I was sure that you would be glad to know—that you would like to congratulate me."

Coryton did not betray the faintest annoyance at this unwelcome intelligence, for which, after

all, he was not unprepared. He simply patted
his friend on the shoulder, as if with encourag-
ing friendliness, and they entered the drawing-
room.

If the noise of a crowd is the best accompaniment
to quiet conversation, as Violet had had the effrontery
to tell Gwendolen, those two young ladies had come
in for an unique opportunity. The game of 'cutlets'
had just come to its usual abrupt termination and
all the players were struggling on their backs
on the floor, emitting peal after peal of uproarious
merriment. The archdeaconess was waggling her
feet and hands, like a beetle on its back waiting
to be turned over; Miss Connecticut was emitting
that shrill transatlantic scream, which is so distressing
to European ears; while Pimlico, who was only
present as a spectator, sat on the edge of the high
fender and panted forth a wild spluttering laugh
that rose and fell in unmusical cadence. Miss
Mudlark put her thumb in her mouth and tried to

look innocent when she perceived that Miss Haviland was among the arrivals. Indeed the latter's presence seemed to act somewhat as a wet blanket upon the high spirits of the party and the hilarity soon died away. as the players gradually regained their feet.

Lady Giddy proposed 'a quieter game', which elicited ribald remarks about the quietness of the preceding one. Pimlico protested that the only quiet game he knew was baccarat. Theodora proposed an adjournment to the billiard-room for pool and Williams moved an amendment, which was seconded by Wilmot, in favour of 'blow-marble' on the billiard-table. but everybody declared they were too much out of breath. Of course Miss Mudlark wanted to have 'blow-marble' explained to her.

"It's very simple," volunteered Violet. 'You pick up sides and then it's like football. The captain blows off the marble and then everybody tries to blow it through the opposite side's goal.

You mayn't touch either the marble or the table during the game. Last time we played it, Pim's and Theo's mouths met in the middle of the table and Lady Elizabeth declares they became so engrossed in each other that they forgot to blow."

There was a general laugh and Theodora shouted, "Shut up, I never play that childish game. Come along, who says pool?"

Everybody was soon streaming along the corridor to the billiard-room and a buzz of conversation went before, like the incense that precedes a procession.

"By the way, Pim, what's become of that bay mare of yours, the Smiler?"—"Gone to the knackers, years ago."—"I met old Wrigglesworth at the Alhambra last week, trying to do the mash."—"Fie! Mr. Coryton, what were you doing at the Alhambra?"—"You don't say so! I am astonished. Known her ever since she was a baby, just about

so high. that's all. "—" He's in luck. Quite good
looking and such a fortune!"—" Yes, such good
fortune with such good looks!"—" According to
the canon law, Lady Elizabeth, a dynasty only
acquires a prescriptive right when a hundred years
have elapsed without a protest."—" Yes, yes, Mr.
Clifford, but what does the agricultural labourer
care about canon law, or indeed any law for the
matter of that?"—" Eight and nine seven times in
succession. I never heard of such a bank."—" Oh!
no one reads newspapers nowadays, least of all the
folks who write them."—" England ceased to be
England when cock-fighting went out of fashion."
—" My dear Mr. Gaverigan, you are hopeless. I
believe you would like us all to go about with
a fig-leaf, because it was the fashion before the
flood."—" Well, some of us do."—" Pray be quiet.
Mrs. Miles will overhear you. She's touchy about
that dress."—" Dress, do you call it?"—" I think
I shall slip off to bed."—"Oh! don't go yet. Pim'll

probably take a bank presently."—"It was a
regular ding-dong finish, and the filly——"—"I
don't believe a word of it."—"Well, I have got
eyes."—"Humph! I hope you haven't got a tongue
too."—"Oh! no, I have not got that."

CHAPTER VI.

A MINISTERIAL RECEPTION.

Tout le monde est assommant. Il n'y a de tolérable
que les gens qui me plaisent, uniquement parce-
qu'ils me plaisent.

—GUY DE MAUPASSANT.

CORYTON had an interview with Lord Southwark
before he left Blarney. A few weeks after, a brief
paragraph found its way into sundry of the Government organs, to the effect that the Marquis of
Southwark had appointed Mr. Walpole Coryton to
be his private secretary.

Coryton entered upon his duties at once. They
were not arduous, for Lord Southwark was by no

119

means an exacting man. The post he held in the
Government was one of great dignity, but small
responsibility. The possession of it entitled the
holder to Cabinet rank and high precedence. The
departmental work was slight, and parliamentary
duties consisted chiefly in piloting Government
measures, about whose passing there could be no
doubt, through the House of Lords, duties which
Lord Southwark performed with admirable grace
and skill. He was a *persona grata* at Court, and
therefore raised no murmur when he was told off,
somewhat frequently, as Minister in attendance.
Those who did not know him, wondered a little
why Lord Southwark went in for politics at all.
He was an enormously wealthy peer, wealthy enough
to buy almost any further honours he might desire,
and great wealth means great influence even in
these days, when pocket-boroughs are not. But
Lord Southwark did not care to buy his honours;
he left that to the " beerage ", and he had some old-

world theories about *noblesse oblige.* So, though he refused the Irish Viceroyalty because it was too much trouble, he accepted this other post, possibly because he courted the blue riband of the Garter, or because he thought that a Cabinet Office—as Prince Bismarck is said to have remarked of the throne of Bulgaria—would always be "a pleasant reminiscence."

Though not exactly the sort of Minister who moulds the destinies of nations, Lord Southwark was an exceedingly clever man, and he liked to have clever people about him. There could be no doubt about Coryton's cleverness; it was evidenced quite as much by what he did not do, as by what he did, and this his chief was quick to find out. Though he did not hold Lord Beaconsfield's views as to the value of private secretaries, and though he was by no means overburdened by generosity— for the generosity of the wealthy is generally in an inverse ratio to their means—Lord Southwark gave Coryton an additional £300 a year to the official £200 accredited him in Whitaker, and a corresponding amount of private work of his own. He also admitted him to a certain degree of his confidence, and with something of the feeling with which one likes to back a winning horse, helped him forward in many little ways.

For Coryton was a winning horse; there could be no doubt of that. He had got his foot firmly planted on the bottom rung of the ladder which leads to fame. He might slip, as many a one has done before, but at present all seemed to go well with him, and he was spoken of everywhere among his friends and acquaintances as a coming man. Others have been spoken of so too, but they are always coming and never come.

Coryton's great obstacle was scarcity of money, but his appointment to Lord Southwark brought him, in these early days, what was almost as good —credit. So with a certain amount of cash in hand

and by making a point of never paying for anything which he could get upon credit, he was able to float along for the present excellently well. This sort of thing could not go on for ever, of course—the day of reckoning must come—but then he would be married to Violet and she could settle his bills.

"That is the truest function of a wife," he thought with an amused smile, as he pictured to himself how enraged Violet would be when she knew the real state of affairs. Their love-affair was a matter of sympathy and interest combined, but the interest played as strong a part in it as the sympathy. "After all," he thought, "what matter? The emotion between the sexes called love is generally part selfish and part animal."

Coryton settled down in London in October, just as town was beginning to fill again a little, and he took chambers on the second floor of a house in Piccadilly overlooking the Green Park. He was

keenly alive to the advantages of a good address
and appearance. He furnished his chambers hand-
somely. partly on credit and partly on the proceeds
of a cheque given to him by that grateful parent
Lord Baltinglass of Blarney. His dress was always
perfect, - it would be so of course with one who
had *carte blanche* at Savile Row; moreover remembering the words of the immortal Mr. Vigo, he
affected a certain slight severity of style which
befitted a budding statesman. He was elected a
member of the Bachelors'. and his name was down
for White's and shortly coming up for the Carlton.
He was always very civil to any journalists who
might come in his way; he paid assiduous court to
Dowagers, and was to be seen regularly at Sunday
morning service at a fashionable church.

He had a good many introductions, of course.
The fact of his being private secretary to a Cabinet
Minister—especially a Minister of Lord Southwark's
social position—was an introduction in itself. He

soon had more invitations than he could accept, and more than he cared for.

"As a rule the people who want to know one are the people one doesn't want to know," he muttered to himself as he tore up two or three dinner invitations which emanated from Kensington-this-side-of-Jordan and threw them into the waste-paper basket. "It is all right to eat these people's dinners," he continued, "but it is a little awkward when one comes across them full-tilt in the Park afterwards. And these sort of people are always in the Park— it is their happy meeting ground—and they never seem to know when you have had enough of them. They should be content to exist for dinner purposes only."

A good many quondam friends of the late Judge-Advocate General turned up again too. They had forgotten all about the son. But now that he seemed to be working his way to the front and was not likely to want anything of them, they came and looked him up, and bade him welcome to their houses.

Coryton accepted their hospitality in the spirit in which it was offered. He could not afford to bear any resentments, even if he had felt them. But he did not. He would have acted in precisely the same way himself under similar circumstances, and his was a philosophy which takes life and human nature as it finds them. 'He who lives for himself lives for but a little thing,' it has been truly said; yet it is very difficult to find anything else to live for.

So the months went by and the fogs came and went, and the dismal thing called Christmas came and went, and the New-Year's bills came and didn't go, and Parliament opened and the Queen's Speech (so-called)—not more ungrammatical than such speeches generally are, and not more stuffed than usual with platitudes and impossible schemes of reform,—was read by a queer little man in a wig and gown whom some called the " Lord High Jobber," and the business of the Session began.

It didn't mean much extra work for Coryton, beyond that he had to keep a sharp eye on the ' Notices for the Day' and to haunt the lobby of the House of Lords four afternoons in the week, or stand below the Bar sometimes when a dull and decorous debate, in which Lord Southwark took part, was going on. The work of a private secretary, whose chief is in the House of Lords—unless that chief should happen to be at the head of a great department—is to a certain extent ornamental, and this part of his duties Coryton was able to fulfil to a nicety, for he posed as a sucking politician to the manner born. It was only on those rare occasions, when he had to attend a debate in the House of Commons, that he felt the full fascination of political life, and heard as it were, the great heart of the nation throb.

Lord Southwark, in addition to his other advantages, possessed a beautiful house and a beautiful wife. The office-seekers and bottle-washers of the Party, who are apt to be envious, said it was these things, rather than his abilities, which had advanced Lord Southwark to so prominent a place in the councils of the nation. It was probably the combination of all these factors, though there might have been some truth in the sneer, for the Party was badly in want of another house whereat to rally its forces. The dreary functions at the Prime Minister's, where people were asked by the letters of the Alphabet, the A's to L's one night, and the M's to Z's another; where the hostess ostentatiously showed her contempt for the greater number of her guests by turning her back upon them and hanging her hand over the banisters to be tugged at like a bell-rope; where the host was wrapped in chilly, unapproachable, Olympian gloom—these functions could scarcely be described as inspiriting. Doubtless though, Mr. Toadey-Snaile, M.P. for

Mudford, and Mrs. Toadey-Snaile, whilom Mayor and Mayoress of that borough, Mr. Creeper Crawley, Editor of the *Lickworm Gazette,* Mr. Hunter Tuft, the society-promoter—and all the other rag-tag and bobtail of the Party were more than consoled for the snubs they had endured by seeing their names in the paper the next morning, and by thinking of the gall and wormwood with which their less favoured friends and intimates would read them there also.

So Lady Southwark, after due consultation with her lord, rose to the occasion and endeavoured to found a political salon. The exclusive portals of Southwark House were opened wide, a miracle in itself, for they were generally shut very close indeed. The Southwarks belonged to the inner circle of what was once considered to be the most exclusive aristocracy in Europe; they formed one of Lady Charles Beresford's famous "forty families" who alone, she says, constitute English society.

"It is a great effort," Lady Southwark confided to Lady Elizabeth Gargoyle, who was a cousin of hers. "These people are not even amusing, they are simply middle-class mediocrities. I am sure that to entertain all those Socialist creatures, Anarchists, and Fenians, and things on the other side would be much more exciting."

"The Devil has all the liveliest tunes, my dear," said Lady Elizabeth. She prided herself on her freedom of speech, and so did her daughter Theodora. "Just think what I go through with those dreadful Primrose League teas, don't you know?"

"Oh! but you are a privileged person," objected Lady Southwark discontentedly, as she scanned her 'to-be-civil' lists. "However, I suppose it can't be helped, Southwark seems to make a point of it and one must do something for one's country."

"Oh! the country isn't in the least danger, I assure you," exclaimed Lady Elizabeth vivaciously. "Are there not the Knights-companion, and the

Harbingers, and the Dames, and the Esquires?
Are not the forces of Clapham and Balham on our
side? As I said the other night to that dear
delightful Radical person—what is his name? He
was in the last Government, you know. I met
him at that Jamrack gathering of Lady Vieille's.
Everyone was there, from a pet Princess to a third-
rate poet—Dear me, Theodora, what was the man's
name? I shall forget my own next."

"Marshall," said Theodora laconically, without
looking up from the poodle she was fondling.

"Marshall—of course, how stupid of me to forget.
'Yes,' I said to him, 'You are a wicked dangerous
man, Mr. Marshall, but we are not a bit afraid of
you, for all the snobs are on our side, you know.'"

"That was a little *mal-à-propos*, wasn't it?"
queried Lady Southwark languidly. "I hear the
creature is going to be married to some colonial
person with social ambitions, and is coming over
to us. The Duchess of Puffeballe has taken him

up. I daresay he will be dining here in the fulness
of time. But then he will have become dull."

" Which is another way of saying he will have
become a good Conservative, you naughty thing,"
said Lady Elizabeth, rising. " Well, we really must
be going. Theodora has to be present at a drawing-
room meeting in aid of broken-down cabrunners,
somewhere in Kensington at five o'clock. Let me
know if you want any additions to your list. Theodora knows all those sort of people, don't you
know, and so do I—only I forget their names.
Theodora doesn't. Good-bye."

Lady Southwark, however, managed her invitations
excellently well without the help of Theodora. Mr.
Coryton came to her assistance instead, and it was
really remarkable, considering the short time he
had been in town, how much he knew about
'those sort of people.' It was not a very difficult
task, they had only to prune down the Prime
Minister's omnium-gatherum lists a little, and the

thing was done, at least so far as the invitations
were concerned. But Lady Southwark was *grande
dame* to her finger-tips and, having made up her
mind to do the thing, she did it well, and had a
gracious smile, and a kindly word for all the motley
throng who pressed up the broad marble staircase
of the Southwark Mansion. She was a perfect
hostess. Ambassadors, diplomats, Peers and Peer-
esses, Bishops and monsignori, Cabinet Ministers,
provincial Tory M.P.'s with their provincial wives
and daughters, and the other odds and ends, who
figure at the tail of a gathering of this kind—all
were welcomed with equal and gracious courtesy.

It was at the last of these receptions, about the
middle of March, that Coryton met Violet again.

He had been dining with Pimlico that evening
and they had been to the Gaiety together on the
strict principle of 'each pay his own.' They
understood one another excellently well, did these two.

"I suppose I'd better show up at my mother's

menagerie, otherwise these things are not much in
my line," said Lord Pimlico superciliously, as they
picked up a hansom in the Strand and rattled
westward together. "But we will go on to the
Stephanotis Club after. In the meantime it will
do to kill an hour."

On his arrival, Pimlico was promptly pounced
upon by Theodora, who had hitherto been joining
in a three-cornered conversation which her mother
was carrying on with the Turkish Ambassador.
She hailed Pimlico with delight and they went off
to talk dogs and horses together, subjects on which
Theodora knew almost as much as he did.

Coryton, left to himself, made his way leisurely
through the crowd and exchanged greetings here
and there. The spacious rooms were very full, for
this was the last reception before Easter and there
was a foreign prince present, whom Lord and Lady
Southwark had entertained at dinner together with
the ambassador who represented the Prince's country,

and other notabilities. Coryton caught sight of the
Prime Minister in the second room standing apart
from the crowd, the Star of the Garter flashing on
his breast, his craggy brow bent forward a little, and
a smile upon his lips as he exchanged a few words
with an extremely pretty girl in a heliotrope gown
caught up with sprays of clematis. It was only
a few words, for the great man's attention was
claimed almost immediately by someone else, and
as he moved away with a bow and a smile the
girl turned also, and Coryton saw that it was
Violet. She caught sight of him at once and greeted
him with a sunny smile.

"Confess," she said, "you are surprised to see
me here."

"And delighted," he replied. "The pleasure is
all the greater because it is unexpected. I had no
idea you were in town."

"I only came up to-day," she said, "and I
knew I should meet you here this evening, so I did

not trouble to let you know. I am staying with Lady Giddy in Seymour Street. She has brought me to night—Oh!" she went on in answer to his questioning glance, "I don't know where she is now. It is impossible to keep close to anyone in the crush; and she disappeared with Wilfrid Tyrconnel five minutes ago. He is here, and Lord Baltinglass too. Quite a meeting of old friends, isn't it? I have been amusing myself quizzing the people and trying to make them out—Come, Poley, find me a seat, and then you shall tell me who they all are."

"I found you talking to the most distinguished of them all," he said, as they made their way into a third and comparatively empty room and sat down on one of the *Louis-seize* couches near the door.

"The Prime Minister—Ah! I knew you would wonder how I came to know him. Well, we met on the Riviera this January—he was there just before Parliament opened—and, do you know? he took rather a fancy to me. So I smiled straight at him when I saw him to-night—it does not do to let oneself be forgotten, he may be useful to us some day. Great men have short memories, is it not so?"

Coryton looked at her admiringly.

"You are a wonderful woman, Vixie," he said.

"And you are a wonderful boy, Poley," she answered. "Oh! I hear about you a good deal. Everyone tells me how fast you are getting on. Together we shall be so wonderful that we shall carry everything before us. And you will soon win fame."

"Fame," he repeated musingly, "that is to be known by people whom you don't know, isn't it?"

"Precisely, Mr. Commonplace Book. But there is nothing better in this life."

"Oh, yes, there is," he said, "to realize the dream of one's youth before one is middle-aged. That is what I shall do when I marry you, Vi."

She looked at him almost affectionately. They were not in the habit of paying one another compliments, these two, but just now each was very much pleased with the other. Perhaps also she cared for him more than a little. She was certainly attracted to him. His physical beauty appealed to her senses and women are always more sensible to such influences than men. Added to which, she thought he was fairly well off—not rich of course —but his income, judging from the style in which he lived—must be a thousand or two a year at the least—or even more, for he might be holding himself in reserve. That was little enough to a young woman of Violet's expensive tastes, but then he was a man who was likely to make more, and win honours besides. Success was written on his brow.

She felt quite proud of him as they talked together and watched the ever-shifting crowd. Lady Giddy was an admirable chaperon,—she left her charge to look after herself.

" You must not realize all your dreams when you marry me, Poley," said Violet presently, harking back to the point at which they started, " or there will be a rude awakening. Our marriage must be the starting point—of fresh opportunities. Everyone has opportunities,—some find them, others make them."

"And some miss them," interpolated Coryton.

" But those are the people who lack either money or brains," she rejoined. " We shall have both."

" True," said Coryton brightening visibly at the mention of the magic word money and pressing the little hand which lay so near his own. " Together we shall do all things. You are my 'affinity' you know, Vi."

She gave a merry laugh and drew her hand away.

" You talk as though you were one of the 'Souls', Poley. Don't try to be sentimental; it doesn't suit you. We are not Gwendolen and her young man, you know."

Coryton acquiesced very philosophically.

" By the way have you seen anything of Gwendolen? " he asked.

Violet pouted.

" Not for ages," she said. " Not since Blarney. But we are to meet in the season, I believe. We correspond—pages. Her letters bore me. The fact is, she bores me too. She is too good for this world. She is only fit for Paradise."

" Poor Paradise," murmured Coryton, " it must be a tiresome place if it be peopled only by those sweet saints whose society we so much dread below."

Violet laughed again. She was always laughing. She had such pretty, pearly teeth.

" It is lucky the Pigeon does not hear you," she exclaimed. " Poor Pigeon! I wonder what Lady Giddy is doing with him all this time .... Oh! here they are. Talk of angels and you hear the rustle of their wings .... What was I laughing at so immoderately, dear Lady Giddy? At those little Orientals over yonder with their backs to the wall. They have been posted there like wax images the whole evening, and such quaint dresses too! Who are they?"

"Some of the staff of the Chinese or Japanese legation most probably," answered Lady Giddy with a careless glance. "Oh! do look at Lady Pfarrerheim, Violet! Did you *ever* see such a sight!"

"Who is Lady Pfarrerheim?"

"That woman near the door in the very *décolletée* dress," replied Lady Giddy, whose own charms were not too closely veiled. "She is one of the *haute Juiverie*. Such an affected creature, enormously rich, but she never wears an atom of jewellery."

"Nor much of anything else it would seem," said Coryton with a laugh. "I have often heard that women dress less to be clothed than to be

adorned, but I never realized it quite so vividly
before."

"She is evidently of opinion that beauty unadorned
is adorned the most," said Violet. "But tell me,
who is the man she has been talking to so earnestly?
Not the Duke of Puffeballe, I know him, but that
other man, with the swarthy face."

"No one much," replied Coryton indifferently.
"One would wonder how he got here, except that
he contrives to push himself everywhere. He is a
professional philanthropist, I believe."

"Dear me," said Lady Giddy waving her fan,
"professional philanthropist! What is that?"

"A man who lives in the West and talks about
the East. It is quite a lucrative profession if one
only talks loud enough. This man has found it
so. As he was very, very poor and obscure he went
in for philanthropy—the cheapest form of advertisement going."

"If he was very poor I don't quite see how he

could help poverty much," said Tyrconnel with a puzzled air. He had talked much about philanthropy with Gwendolen, and their schemes always meant spending a good deal of money.

"Oh! it is quite easy," said Coryton. "If you have no money of your own, you are charitable at the expense of other people. You get just the same amount of credit—rather more in point of fact. It is merely an extended application of the saying of Sydney Smith's. A. never sees B. in trouble, without thinking that C. ought to help him . . . . . But come, Vixie, shall we go downstairs? People are beginning to go. The crush will be over now."

In the supper-room they came across Theodora and Pimlico. That youth was evidently impatient to be gone, and asked Coryton if he wasn't ready to "make tracks."

"That is very rude of you, when you see he is with me," said Violet.

"Yes, but you are going to make tracks too, aren't you? There is nothing to do. If there were only a sit-down supper, it would be something—but this sort of thing,"—here he gave a contemptuous glance in the direction of the long buffet—"Why my mother fills her house with all sorts of bounders she doesn't know anything about, fairly stumps me.... More fiz, Theo? No? Then let me put your glass down."

"It is certainly very decorous and very dull," laughed Violet. "Even the gowns are all of a Lenten hue. If there had only been some music, it would have helped us on a little. Conversation, I fear me, is a lost art. However, I have accomplished what I came for, which was to have a chat with you, Poley, and now I must be going, for I see Lady Giddy looking towards us. We shall be in at five to-morrow, don't forget."

"You are coming with Corry and me, Pigeon, aren't you?" queried Pimlico a few minutes later.

They were all three standing together, cloaked and hatted, in the vestibule, waiting for a hansom.

"It is the first I have heard about it," rejoined Tyrconnel. "Where are you going?"

"To the Stephanotis for an hour or so,—just to take the taste of this sort of thing out of our mouths."

"I—I—am afraid it's a little late. I think I shall turn in," stammered Tyrconnel irresolutely.

"It is not half-past twelve yet," said Coryton, "but as you please, of course."

"What rot!" ejaculated Pimlico—"I can't think what's come over you, Pigeon. Why, there'll be a lot of fellows there you know—Gaverigan, Forbes, all the rest of them—and I daresay Pussie Prancewell too, and Sally Popkins."

A swift change swept over Tyrconnel's face at the mention of the latter name.

"I am sorry," he said decidedly, "but I cannot come." He looked towards Coryton as he spoke.

Coryton said nothing.

" Well," exclaimed Pimlico in a huff, " if you won't, you won't. *I* don't care. Come on, Corry, we can't wait about here all night. If we walk a few steps we shall pick up a hansom."

Nevertheless when they were bowling down Piccadilly, he returned again to the subject.

" I can't think what's come over Pigeon. He's quite a different chap to what he used to be. Is he going in for piety, or what? "

" He is going in for matrimony—with a good girl," said Coryton quietly, lighting a cigarette.

CHAPTER VII.

AT THE LEVEE.

'Vanity of vanities,' saith the
    preacher, 'Vanity of vanities,
    all is vanity.'
                    —ECCLESIASTES.

IT was a little before two o'clock on a sunny
May afternoon. There was an air of subdued
excitement in the vicinity of Marlborough House
and St. James's Palace, and a gaping crowd of the
vulgar had gathered itself together at the corner
of Pall Mall; a crowd which extended up St.
James's Street in one direction, and down towards
the Park in the other. For the Prince of Wales

147

was about to hold a Levee by command of the Queen, and the street was bright with uniforms and an incessant stream of vehicles was driving up the side entrance of St. James's Palace. The crowd, with that love of "dressing up" which seems inherent in the human race, looked on and gaped.

Among the men who rattled up in a hansom was Coryton, wearing a regulation black velvet suit. He entered the Palace, and having handed one of his two cards to the gorgeous being in the corridor known as the Queen's Page, went up the stairs and found himself in the midst of a panting, pushing crowd in the outermost ante-room.

It was a largely attended Levee—more than usually so, for there had been a Royal wedding, or some such event, and loyal subjects were more than usually eager to pay their respects to their Sovereign.

It was an odd spectacle. A number of commonplace and estimable elderly gentlemen had impaired their digestions by hurrying over an early luncheon, and had made themselves uncomfortable by arraying themselves in sundry unusual and grotesque garments, in which they vainly strove to look as little ridiculous as possible.

There was a worthy old country squire, for instance, who had never before ventured on any colour but 'pink,' masquerading in the gorgeous apparel of a Deputy-Lieutenant; there was a High Sheriff, whose attenuated legs were never meant for silk stockings, but who had donned them in order to be presented by the Lord Lieutenant of his county. We say 'his county' with reserve, for he hadn't much to do with it, albeit he was High Sheriff. The evolution of a High Sheriff nowadays is a comparatively rapid process. A wealthy stock-jobber or something of that ilk, buys a place in the country,—not much of a place necessarily—but he must have plenty of ready cash. He restores

a church perchance, subscribes liberally to the
hounds and local charities, and then the Lord
Lieutenant gets him put on the county bench.
In a very short time he will be 'pricked' for
the office of High Sheriff of his county, though
he may have known nothing about the county ten
years before. Is it small wonder, under the circumstances, that the impecunious but *bona fide* country
gentlemen are agitating for the abolition of this
once honoured office?

There was a stout old general, puffing and blowing
in a uniform, which was very much too tight for
him now. There was an endless variety of uniforms,
varied here and there by the black gowns and
Geneva bands of a sprinkling of ecclesiastics, and
by the sober court-dresses of the civilians. There
were several Orientals present too, whose gaudy
raiment gave a touch of colour to the scene. There
was in fact the usual collection of somebodies and
nobodies—though, as most of the somebodies

enjoyed the privilege of the *entrée*, the nobodies predominated here.

Conspicuous among them was the well-known "Society-promoter" Mr. Hunter Tuft who had religiously attended Levees for years in the vain hope of favours to come, but had never received the slightest recognition from the Court—not even an invitation to a Marlborough House Garden-party. Poor Hunter Tuft! he was no nearer his cherished goal now, than when he commenced his upward career in Kensington-beyond-Jordan, twenty years ago. All the same he entertained ambassadors and ambassadresses at his club and was an adjunct to every fashionable wedding in Belgravia. He consoled himself for Court neglect by saying airily, "The Marlborough House set is so very mixed, you know." The Royal favour is ever to the sour grapes to the many, sweet few.

Mr. Toadey-Snaile M.P. was also here of course, and many other M.P.'s of the same kidney, who

take care that their presence at the Levee is duly
chronicled in the local papers of their respective
constituencies.   It all tends to help them with the
Knights and Dames of Primrose Habitations, or
with   the   Radicals   who   love   a   lord—often   the
greatest snobs of all.   Here was Creeper Crawley,
who had managed to crawl in by the backdoor
somehow.   He represented Letters perchance, since
the more eminent men in that line were conspicuous
by their absence.   Here was our old friend Sir
Cincinnatus Spreadeagle clad in a gaudy Militia
uniform, prepared to shed the last drop of his blood
in defence of his Queen and country, as he said in
that never-to-be-forgotten after-dinner speech in the
House of Commons.   They were all here, kicking
their heels and chattering glibly to one another.

Coryton saw a good many faces he knew, as
he looked around and pressed slowly onward, urged
forward by the ever increasing crowd behind.   Suddenly he espied a familiar form arrayed in an

unfamiliar garb. It was Tyrconnel. His back was towards Coryton. He was apparently looking blankly at the quaint tapestry on the wall, but he turned round quickly as Coryton tapped him on the shoulder and asked:

"*Que diable, Pigeon, viens-tu faire dans cette galère?*"

"I might return the question," rejoined Tyrconnel, smiling all over his face at this unexpected meeting.

"I—oh! it's my first appearance," said Coryton. "Lord Southwark is presenting me."

"I haven't been to a Levee this year and my father insisted on my showing up at this one. Not that it makes the slightest difference to anyone whether I do so or not—and it's a horrid bore," said Tyrconnel, ruefully, trying to disentangle his sword from between his legs.

"An imperative duty, the patriotic Spreadeagle would tell you," corrected Coryton. "See how important he looks. As for Creeper Crawley yonder, it is the proudest moment of his life."

" It is one of the most uncomfortable moments of mine," panted Tyrconnel, " the heat is awful —I wish they would open the windows."

" We must suffer to be beautiful," laughed Coryton. " What are you doing this afternoon? shall we drive to Ranelagh later and dine quietly together? "

" I—I—am going to see Gwen," replied the other, " she's in town, you know. They came up last week."

"Oh, is she?" said Coryton, raising his eyebrows ever so slightly. " I should like to see her too." He had reasons for being amiable to Gwendolen. " May I come with you? I can take charge of Mrs. de Courcy Miles."

" Do, by all means," exclaimed Tyrconnel, his face brightening. " To tell you the truth, that old woman is an awful trial. She is always pestering

me with questions about Lord This and Lady That
—I can hardly get in a word with Gwen edgeways."

"Old woman indeed!" laughed Coryton, "it is
lucky for your *beaux yeux* she doesn't hear you.
However, I will simply satiate her with the Peerage
if it pleases you. It's all in a day's work. By
Jove!" as they were urged forward. "What a
crowd there is! We shall go past the Prince at a
trot I expect."

"When we get to him. We've got to squeeze
through two or three more rooms first," said Tyrconnel resignedly. "The dodge I believe is to
come late and then one can simply walk through
the rooms at the tail of the procession without any
delay at all. That is what Forbes says he does;
but one day he cut it too fine and found the whole
show over, and the palace shut up. But hark!"
as the sound of music floated up from below.

"Here is the Prince arriving, the crush will soon
ease itself now."

Half an hour later they were both standing under the old gateway of St. James's Palace.

"What a pity you tripped over your sword at the supreme moment, Pigeon," said Coryton cruelly. "You made quite a sensation. I shouldn't be surprised if you find yourself figuring in the comic papers. However, it's over now. Let us walk up the street a little way and hail a hansom. It's no use waiting here. As soon as I have changed these togs I will come round with you. No; on second thoughts, I'll follow you later. Where are they staying?"

"405B, Park Street," said the crestfallen Tyrconnel, ruefully regarding his damaged sword. "But you don't mean what you said about the comic papers, do you, old man—I hate being laughed at."

"No, it was only my fun, that'll be all right, laughed Coryton reassuringly—"Here's a hansom. Jump in, and let's get out of this gaping crowd."

CHAPTER VIII.

MRS. MILES'S SEASON.

'While tumbling down the turbid stream,
Lord love us, how we apples swim!'
—DAVID MALLETT.

'What a monstrous tail our cat has got!'
—HENRY CAREY.

MRS. DE COURCY MILES had come up to town for the
season and had brought Gwendolen with her. She
was in the habit of coming to town for the season,
albeit in a general way the season and Mrs. de
Courcy Miles had about as much to do with one
another as the groves of Camberwell have to do
with the gilded saloons of Mayfair. But this year

157

Mrs. de Courcy Miles had hooked herself on to the skirts of Mayfair; that is to say she had sufficiently moved up in the world to hire three rooms on the second floor of a house in the little street which runs along the back of Park Lane, and which may be therefore said to have a sort of illegitimate relationship with that aristocratic region. True, the house in question abutted on Oxford Street, but Mrs. Miles, who knew the value of a good address, duly announced herself and Miss Haviland as 'arriving at 405B Park Street, Grosvenor Square, for the season.' The announcement was not of the faintest possible interest to anyone save Mrs. Miles herself, and perhaps a few Cambridge and Kensington-beyond-Jordan friends, who not knowing the precise geographical position of 405B, gnashed their teeth with impotent spleen and wondered 'how that woman did it'.

Mrs. Miles, moreover, followed up the announcement by driving round in a hired brougham and leaving her cards on every imaginable person with whom she could by any possibility consider herself to be on calling terms. These tactics combined with rumours of the coming Baltinglass alliance, secured a certain number of invitations, issued more on Gwendolen's account than on her own. In fact, it seemed to Mrs. Miles that they were launched on a perfect whirl of dissipation.

Her other seasons, truth to tell—though she would have died rather than own it even to herself—had not been altogether a success.

"I really could not exist without my London season, it does brush away the provincial cobwebs so," she was in the habit of telling her Cambridge friends. Then she would launch forth into descriptions of sundry smart parties, of which she knew nothing but what the papers told her.

Her Cambridge friends, who knew even less than she, could not contradict her. But it was all imaginary. Mrs. Miles's 'season' consisted in point of fact of three

weeks in a second-rate lodging in a second-rate
street, of frequent promenades in the Park and a
religious attendance of church parade, of sundry
exhibitions, of a close inspection of shopwindows, a
few theatres, a visit to the Academy—all these
sort of people always go to the Academy—and
possibly a tea or two in Bayswater or Kensington.
Then she returned to Cambridge, and declared herself
utterly done up with the fatigues of her 'season.'

But this year she was more successful. She had
squeezed an extra £100 out of the Professor and
brought up Gwendolen. The Baltinglasses were
not much good from a social point of view in
spite of their wealth—a fact surely more due to
Miss Tyrconnel's Evangelical opinions than to Lord
Baltinglass's vulgarity—for society will swallow
any pill if it be only sufficiently gilded. But Lady
Giddy helped somewhat, with an eye to future
possibilities, and that doubtless also accounted for
many of the invitations which found their way to

405B Park Street, Grosvenor Square. The Grosvenor Square was never forgotten. Mrs. Miles even ran to gold-stamped paper in its honour. She was regarding it lovingly now, as she answered a dinner invitation, which had just come from Miss Tyrconnel.

"Such a good address, and so near the Park too," she said aloud as she closed the envelope. Of course it was stamped on the flap as well.

"It is nearer the Marble Arch," said Gwendolen bluntly. She was looking out, over the boxes of geranium and lady-slipper in the window.

Mrs. de Courcy Miles looked up irritably. She objected to Gwendolen's bald way of putting things.

"Do come away and shut down that window a little," she exclaimed; "I am sure the smell of the lunch must be out of the room by now. Have you put the photographs and the flowers on the table again? Yes, that's right, and the *World*, please, and the *Morning Post*, and a book or two, and the Red Book—pray, Gwendolen, do not forget the Red Book and the Peerage. There now, we will just arrange the chairs a little, and no one will know but that it is a drawing-room only."

"What does it matter whether they know it or not?" said Gwendolen a little wearily.

"Matter!" exclaimed Mrs. Miles shrilly, "of course it matters a very great deal. It is past three o'clock and people might be dropping in any minute."

"And they might not," rejoined Gwendolen drily, with a remembrance born of previous experience.

"And they might not," repeated Mrs. Miles unmoved, "but in any case we must be prepared. And I thought you said Wilfrid Tyrconnel was coming on here after the Levee. I wonder you have not more proper pride, Gwendolen. You forget that we owe a duty to society, you the future Lady Baltinglass of Blarney."

"That is nothing to me—nothing," exclaimed Gwendolen, her face flushing. "I am tired of hearing about it. I am tired of this make-believe and pretence. The title is nothing, the money is nothing. I would marry Wilfrid just as willingly —aye, more so—if he had not a penny in the world."

"You are quite right to tell him so, dear," rejoined Mrs. de Courcy Miles approvingly, "but you needn't waste it upon *me*. Please give me the third volume of 'Lady Ermyntrude's Folly.' It is on the table yonder. We needn't talk any more until somebody comes."

So settling herself down in the most comfortable chair, Mrs. Miles was soon lost in her society novel, so-called. It was one of the voluminous series of a well-known lady novelist, who has never viewed society, properly understood, from any nearer point of view than the area railings.

It was not very long before Tyrconnel arrived. He was followed closely by Coryton, who rescued him from Mrs. de Courcy Miles's clutches, and engaged the whole of that lady's attention by whispering to her certain coming scandals among the upper ten thousand, which he manufactured as he went along, but which Mrs. Miles listened to as attentively as if they were gospel, in fact a good deal more so.

This gave Tyrconnel and Gwendolen the opportunity they were longing for—a quiet chat together. They withdrew to the shelter of the window-seat and were soon recounting all their thoughts and experiences since last they met, just as though they had not already confided everything to each other in closely written pages of Bath post—six sheets in a budget.

Then they began to discuss their plans. Gwendolen was quite a country cousin, she had so many things she wished to see—two or three plays, *Olivia* for one, and the summer exhibition at the New Gallery. Then she wanted to go to the morning service at Westminster Abbey next Sun-

day,—would Wilfrid come? They had tickets from
the Dean for the choir. And there were several
parties she didn't care much about, save for the
chance of meeting him at them, and there was a
philanthropic meeting at Crowther Lodge in aid
of little Italian children. She didn't know much
about Italian children—organ grinders or otherwise
—but she would like to go. Would Wilfrid go
with her there too? Of course; he would follow
her into the lion's mouth if need be.

Then they began to talk about their engagement,
which had not yet been publicly announced, though
it was an open secret among their acquaintances.

" Was Lord Baltinglass more reconciled to it? "
she asked timidly. She had only seen him once
since they came to town, but Miss Tyrconnel was
on their side.

" And we have to thank Coryton too," said
Tyrconnel, " he has great influence with the Guv'nor
and has quite talked him round. Oh! yes, there

is no longer any obstacle to fear from that quarter. The Guv'nor doesn't like to seem to give his consent too quickly, but he has given it and he's not a man to go back from his word, whatever his faults may be. You see, it will be announced before the end of the season."

"I do not care anything about the announcement," she said, "if only you do not mind waiting for me, Wilfrid."

"Dear one," he said. clasping her hands, "I would wait for you twice seven years, if need be, as Jacob waited for Rachel."

She looked at his flushed and eager face, a great light of trust and love shining in her eyes. The little breeze from the scarcely closed window ruffled her hair about her brow and wafted in a faint fragrance of musk upon the summer air. The shabby room was transformed into an enchanted palace for these two.

Meanwhile Mrs. de Courcy Miles having listened

with great relish to a description of the Duchess
of Puffeballe's dance which she determined to
transcribe on paper (as an eye-witness) at the
earliest opportunity for the benefit of the wife of
the Vice-Chancellor, descended suddenly to matters
more personal. After a side-glance towards the
two in the window she asked Coryton in a lowered
voice much the same question as the one Gwendolen had already put to Tyrconnel, though from
very different motives.

"I think the engagement ought to be announced
without delay," she said. "I presume Lord Baltinglass has no objections now that his consent has
been virtually given. Have you seen him lately?"

"I met him in the lobby of the House of
Lords the other afternoon," replied Coryton in the
same confidential tones, "and we talked upon the
subject at some length. As you are aware, Lord
Baltinglass is much prepossessed in Miss Haviland's
favour, and he has no serious objections to urge;

still it is only right for me to tell you that he thinks his son might have looked higher, and——"

"I am sure Gwendolen is qualified to hold her own in any society," interrupted Mrs. Miles tartly, for the objection sounded like a reflection on herself; "which is more than can be said of Lord Baltinglass. What more can the man want?"

"I have no doubt about that," said Coryton, blandly, in his most ultra-Parliamentary manner. "She does indeed, in the highest degree, reflect credit upon your admirable training. One cannot say more than that. But it appears that Lord Baltinglass, after the manner of his kind, had cherished the ambition of his son's allying himself with some great house, and it is the idea of his having to forego this ambition, which has been displeasing to him."

Coryton had reasons of his own for magnifying Lord Baltinglass's reluctance. Mrs. de Courcy Miles looked somewhat blank, though visibly mollified at the compliments paid to her.

"We are dining at Baltinglass House on the 21st," she said.

"I am glad to hear it," said Coryton; "it proves that the conversation between Lord Baltinglass and myself has not been barren of results. As I was about to remark, Lord Baltinglass has now determined to cordially consent to the marriage. He has, as I said before, the highest opinion of Miss Haviland. Her beauty and grace, no less than her sound common-sense, have made a great impression on him, and he is anxious that Wilfrid should marry young and sow his wild oats. Lord Baltinglass is not one who looks lightly on youthful follies, nor, need I add, does Miss Tyrconnel. They think an early marriage will be his salvation, and Lord Baltinglass is anxious that there should be no lack of heirs to perpetuate his name. I myself think it is the best thing to be done, for, of course, as you are aware, Lord Baltinglass's vast fortune is entirely at his own disposal and he is just the sort of man, if angered by some youthful indiscretion, to disinherit Wilfrid."

"He cannot keep him out of the title," said Mrs. Miles.

"True," said Coryton drily, "but a title without money is but little worth—especially a brand-new one. It is difficult for an empty bag to stand upright. However, we will not contemplate such a possibility. I only mention it now, as an additional reason for hurrying on the marriage."

"I am sure we are all very much obliged to you, Mr. Coryton," said his listener with effusion.

"Pray do not mention it," he replied with a deprecatory smile, "I am only too glad to be of any little service to my friends, and——"

What he might have added was never uttered, for at that moment a heavy footstep was heard ascending the stairs, and then, to everyone's astonishment, the Professor entered the room.

CHAPTER IX.

THE PLUCKING OF THE PROFESSOR.

'Professors are admirable persons so long
as they confine themselves strictly to the
subjects which they profess.'—LORD R.
CHURCHILL: Speech at the University
Carlton Club Dinner, Cambridge, June 1885.

THE Professor seemed unusually flustered and
hurried. One hand grasped a carpet-bag and the
other the University Don's inevitable umbrella.
His broad-brimmed hat was brushed the wrong .
way. Something had evidently occurred to startle
him out of his normal, professorial calm.

"Goodness gracious, James!" exclaimed Mrs.

171

Miles, viewing the unexpected visitant with an inhospitable eye. "Whatever brings you here—bursting in upon us like this?"

The Professor did not hear her apparently. He removed his hat and put it upon the table. Then he saluted Gwendolen solemnly on either cheek, and would have performed a similar ceremony with his sister, had not that lady adroitly avoided it.

"Can I get a bed here to-night, Maria?" he asked in his usual strident tone, after he had shaken hands with the two young men.

Mrs. Miles shuddered. That vulgar name! She always signed herself 'Marie.'

"Well, yes, I suppose so," she rejoined ungraciously. "If you don't mind going up rather high, that is to say," she added, her thoughts running on a certain little attic up among the tiles.

The Professor looked somewhat doubtful. He knew that attic.

"You can have my room, father," broke in Gwendolen, coming forward and taking him affectionately by the arm.

"Your room! Good gracious! Gwendolen, what are you thinking about?" exclaimed Mrs. Miles sharply. "There's the ball to-night. Who is going to move all your things, I should like to know, and how are you going to manage to dress properly up in that little garret? I won't have you crowding in with me, so don't think it."

Then she paused abruptly, remembering that these domestic details were hardly suitable for discussion before her visitors. To divert attention she turned on the Professor again.

"James," she repeated, "*will* you tell me what has brought you up to town in this unexpected manner?"

"Business, my dear, business," rejoined the Professor, sitting down and wiping his spectacles deliberately, "urgent and important business.

I had a letter from my broker this morning to
say that the Vald'oro Gold Mines were in a very
shaky condition, so I wired to him to sell out at
once and followed up my telegram in person to
see if I cannot find a suitable investment for those
two or three thousand pounds. Nothing like being
prompt in these matters," he said looking towards
Coryton, with that business-like air which very
unbusiness-like people are so fond of assuming.

"Nothing indeed, I quite agree with you," replied
Coryton, his eyes glistering at the mention of
those two or three thousand pounds.

"Humph!" ejaculated Mrs. Miles, whose opinion
of her brother's business capacities was by no
means high. "I hope you won't be taken in, James."

"My dear," rebuked the Professor loftily. "I
am always guided by the advice of my brokers.
Though I confess," he added with a momentary
hesitation, "they have not always advised me
aright."

"Hardly, if they advised Vald'oro Gold Mines,"
interpolated Coryton with an affectation of superior
knowledge. "May I ask who are your brokers,
Professor Haviland?"

"Messrs. Grabbit and Shark," replied the Professor. "What! Do you know anything about
them?"

"I would rather not say what I know about
them," replied Coryton, with commendable caution
considering that he knew nothing at all. Then
he continued, with the air of one who could say
much, an he would: "But, as you know, my
position gives me many opportunities of seeing
behind the scenes—and if I might venture to
advise, I should strongly recommend you not to
consult them with reference to future investments.
I must not say more—I must not indeed. What
I have been told was in the strictest confidence,
but my information came from the highest sources—I
cannot say more."

"There, James, you hear," broke in Mrs. de Courcy Miles. "Mr. Coryton is the Marquis of Southwark's private secretary and his warning is not to be lightly put aside. What have I always told you about Grabbit and Shark? You know how they let you in over that Lofosz business as well as these Vald'oro Mines."

"Really, Maria," said the Professor, "if you remember you counselled the Lofosz investment yourself."

But he was frightened at Coryton's words. All people who dabble in doubtful speculations are apt to be at the merest breath of suspicion.

"What do you advise then, Mr. Coryton?" he queried, addressing him with increased respect.

"I only wished to warn you as a friend," replied Coryton with assumed reluctance. "To advise you further is another matter. Of course you know"—this to Mrs. de Courcy Miles—"Lord Southwark invests largely of his surplus income every month." The lady bowed assent. "I have therefore many opportunities of getting the 'straight tip' so to speak, which are debarred to the million; still I hardly know if I should be justified in——"

"Oh! do please advise James, dear Mr. Coryton," cried Mrs. de Courcy Miles, as he paused. "You don't know what a child he is in business matters. Yes, you are, James, there's no denying it. Do tell him of some nice safe investment with a good interest. Anything which Lord Southwark has money in must, I am sure, be first-class."

"Well, I don't know that I ought to do so," said Coryton lowering his voice to suit the solemnity of the occasion. "Were it anyone but you I should refuse; but I can refuse you nothing.... Well then," he went on in a lowered voice as though he were imparting a Cabinet secret, "a Company has just been formed—the shares are only just on the market—to promote one of the

greatest inventions the world has ever seen. There
is a great future before it—absolute security—and
20% dividend on the first half year. The 'Patent
Automatic Drainage Company' it is called. For
obvious reasons I do not care to explain the details
just now, but it is a marvellously good investment.
Lord Southwark thinks most highly of it."

"And is Lord Southwark one of the directors?"
queried Mrs. Miles, her eyes brightening at the
prospect of that 20% dividend.

"Lord Southwark does not see his way to
becoming a director at present," replied Coryton
with gentle rebuke. "He has to consider his
position in the Ministry—but he is greatly interested," (In point of fact Lord Southwark had no
more to do with it than the man in the moon),
"and in a small way, comparatively speaking, I
am interested myself. But the Board of Directors
is a very influential one. It includes the Marquis
of Swindleycate, the Earl of Bubbelfraude, Lord

Guineapygge, Sir Hawke Pluckpigeon K.C.B., Alder-
man Sir Levi Lazarus, Mr. Toadey-Snaile M.P. and
many other names wellknown in the world of finance."

"There, James," cried Mrs. de Courcy Miles,
quite overcome by this illustrious list. "What
better guarantees can you have? Please talk the
matter over with Mr. Coryton. How providential
you should have met him in this way. But"—her
thoughts reverting to the original grievance—"I
must say it is very inconsiderate of you to rush
in upon us without notice in this way, we have
so much going on too. Gwendolen dear, what are
our engagements for this evening?"

During the whole of this colloquy Gwendolen
and her lover had been engrossed with one another on the window-seat. Mrs. Miles found it
necessary to repeat the question.

"Surely, Aunt, you know—we have not so many
engagements," replied her uncomfortably truthful
niece.

Mrs. Miles wisely ignored the rebuke and consulted her tablets.

"Ah! yes," she said, "it is as I thought. We are dining at Lady Giddy's and going on to Mrs. Connecticut's ball afterwards. You see, James, how inconsiderate you are. I have ordered no dinner. You'll get nothing here."

"Perhaps Professor Haviland will come and dine with me quite quietly at my club," suggested Coryton. "It would give me great pleasure if he would."

"That would be very nice," said Mrs. de Courcy Miles accepting for the Professor promptly, "and then you might have a little business chat together."

Gwendolen gave Coryton a grateful glance. She was always grateful for any little kindness to her father. She was very fond of him and resented the way in which Mrs. Miles was apt to shunt him aside.

"Well, I must be going," said Coryton taking

up his hat. " We shall meet at eight then, Professor. So good of you to say you will come. Are you coming my way, Tyrconnel? "

"I think so," he replied, for he saw that as Coryton was leaving all chances of a further *tête-à-tête* were over. " We shall meet at Mrs. Connecticut's, Gwendolen. Oh! there is one thing I wanted to ask you—I had almost forgotten it. Will you and Mrs. Miles drive down with us to Hurlingham next Saturday and have lunch there? There is to be a Meet of the Four-in-hand first of all, don't you know, and the idea was that we should drive down on Pimlico's coach."

" Delightful! " exclaimed Mrs. Miles with rapture. " We should love it of all things."

She had often been among the crowd which watches the Meets of the Coaching Club and Four-in-Hand from the footpaths. Now she was to be on a coach instead. Surely her ambitions were being realized at last. " Oh! how I hope the

Overdone-Jones's will be there to see!" she thought to herself.

But Gwendolen demurred.

"I do not like Lord Pimlico," she said, flushing a little. Poor Pimlico was the scapegoat just now, her suspicions having been diverted from Coryton. She in fact regarded him as Wilfrid's evil genius, *vice* Coryton promoted.

"What nonsense!" said Mrs. Miles, "I think Lord Pimlico a most charming person, his manners are the perfection of *haut ton;* as indeed they would be—the eldest son of the Marquis of South-wark. Really, Gwendolen, you are too ridiculous. I suppose there will be a large party, Mr. Tyr-connel?"

"No," said Coryton answering for him. "Pimlico doesn't care about crowding his coach. I don't know how many exactly; but Lady Elizabeth and Miss Gargoyle, Lady Giddy and Miss Tresillian and two or three men are coming, I believe."

"There, do you hear, Gwendolen?" said Mrs. Miles. "Lady Elizabeth Gargoyle is going. Really, you are a little too absurd!"

"I thought Gwendolen would like to come," said Tyrconnel a little hurt 'but of course if she doesn't, we will say no more about it."

Gwendolen looked distressed. She heeded Mrs. de Courcy Miles's railings no more than the flies upon the wall, but she did not wish to hurt Wilfrid's feelings, just when they were so happy together. Perhaps after all she was carrying her dislike of Lord Pimlico too far. She gave Tyrconnel her hand.

"I will come with pleasure if you wish it," she said.

The Professor dined that evening with Coryton as arranged. They had a nice little dinner and a really excellent bottle of port, to which the Professor, as befitted a University Don, did ample

justice. Only Mr. Toadey-Snaile, that notorious
Guinea-pig, dined with them before going down
to the House. Coryton couldn't get any other
members of the Syndicate together at so short a
notice, but Mr. Snaile served excellently well.
Before the evening was over the Professor had
quite determined to invest his odd thousands in the
Automatic Drainage Company—which Coryton was
floating with a few titled decoys—and even to sell
out other stock for the same purpose. Such an
opportunity, as both Coryton and Mr. Snaile impressed upon him, was not to be lost. The younger
gentleman was comparatively new to the art of
company-promoting, but he played his part to the
manner born—so much so as to evoke the involuntary
admiration of that old fox, Toadey-Snaile. No one
knew how to pluck a pigeon better than Coryton,
his early training admirably fitted him for the work
and the Professor was the silliest of all pigeons—
one who thinks himself wise. University dons,

old women, and country parsons, are notoriously
the worst at business. It is upon them that bubble
speculators, financial agents, company-promoters
and such-like vermin, fatten and flourish. Someone
has said the world is made up of knaves and
fools—mostly fools. This is perhaps an arbitrary
division, the one thing certain is that there is a
continual transference going on from the pockets
of those who have money, to the pockets of those
who have it not.

The starving man who steals a roll from a
baker's shop is punished with the utmost rigour
of the law, but such as these who devour widows'
houses and for pretence make long prayers, go
scot-free, and live and die in the odour of sanctity.
The shadow of the Green Bay Tree is over them all.

A merry party drove down to Hurlingham the
following Saturday. It was a beautiful sunshiny
morning with just enough breeze to temper the

heat. A little rain had fallen during the night, not much, but enough to freshen the trees in the Park and render the water-carts unnecessary. Pimlico kept his team of bays together in fine style, and handled the ribbons in masterful manner, evoking the noisy admiration of Theodora, who occupied the box seat and gave her opinion on the points of the horses in that delightfully candid and professional manner for which she was renowned. Mrs. de Courcy Miles had the audacity to manœuvre for the box-seat herself, but Theodora soon settled that. However, Mrs. Miles managed to make herself very much at home elsewhere, and even had the satisfaction of espying the Overdone-Jones's gaping at her from the path—just a little way below the Magazine. Miss Tresillian was unable to come; she was knocked up after last night's ball, she had written; but the real truth of the matter was that her dress did not come home in time—a ravishing creation of Kate Reilly's—

and she had 'nothing to wear.' However, she bore the disappointment very philosophically by taking it out in bed—with a French novel and a big box of bon-bons. Her 'dear Poley' would console himself, no doubt.

A dainty little luncheon was awaiting them at the other end, a meal fit for Lucullus; though probably Lucullus, like most of those who make dining one of the fine arts, would have voted luncheon a mistake. When it was over, later in the afternoon the 'all and sundry' as Theodora phrased it began to troop in.

"It is always so fresh and delightful here," said Lady Giddy to Coryton with a comprehensive wave of her parasol at the velvet turf and shady trees, "that I feel quite good. One's surroundings have a good deal to do with one's feeling good; don't you think?"

"Possibly," said Coryton with a glance at the animated crowd, "though I confess Hurlingham never struck me in a pastoral light before. But then whatever our sins may be, we always flatter ourselves that we are conquering them—even when they are conquering us."

Lady Giddy laughed. "You are incorrigible," she said. "We will talk of something more interesting. Let us come and look at the Polo."

So they went and sat near the queer, mushroom-shaped little tents, and watched the game and listened to the music of the band. Coryton naturally translated 'something more interesting' to mean Lady Giddy herself. So he chose the most subtle form of flattery and talked to her about herself. Lady Giddy was not backward in responding and they were soon embarked on the initial stages of a flirtation. However, they did not get very far ahead to-day, for the coaches began to move away early, as they generally do. Theodora was looking forward to the homeward drive and Pimlico was impatient to be gone. Gwendolen and Tyrconnel were hunted up with difficulty by Mrs. de Courcy Miles. They had turned their backs on the Polo, had gone off somewhere together in the grounds. But they were captured at last; and then the whole party drove homeward before the trees began to cast long shadows.

CHAPTER X.

HENLEY REGATTA.

The virtue of widows is a laborious virtue:
they have to combat constantly with the
remembrance of past bliss.
—St. Jerome.

THE season was waning fast. Each year it seems
to die harder and to take longer about it; but it
was dying at last,—there could be no doubt about
that. The trees in the Park were dusty and
grimy; the flower-boxes in the windows of Belgravia
and Mayfair had lost their freshness and it was
too late for people to think of renewing them;
the streets and squares were stuffy and hot. There

was an air of finality about everything, people pined for a breath of fresh country air. Society generally was pluming itself for flight—discussing the possibilities of Goodwood and Cowes, where it would meet once more before dispersing itself to Homburg waters or Scottish moors.

The Eton and Harrow Match, the turning point of a dying season, was just over and Lady Giddy had gone down to her place near Henley to entertain a party of friends for the Regatta. Not that Lady Giddy cared about the Regatta; she had been to so many and they were all alike; but it served as a peg to hang a house-party on.

Lady Giddy had a pretty little place on the river about a mile below Henley Bridge; a spacious house in good-sized grounds, the verdant lawns of which sloped down to the water's edge, beneath umbrageous trees. There was a tiny park and a charming boat-house. The house itself faced the river against a back-ground of beech trees, which were wont to don wondrous autumn tints of brown and red and gold.

People who did not know Lady Giddy very well often wondered why she did not marry again. People who knew her better did not wonder at all. Her late husband, an old Indian Judge and K.C.S.I., whom she had married for his money, became aware of the fact that she had done so, and, being of a jealous disposition, he willed his property in such a manner that everything would leave her if she married again.

So his young and handsome widow was left to perform an involuntary suttee. Her moneyed admirers did not admire her enough to marry her for her own sake, and the impecunious ones were out of the question. Love in a cottage would not suit Lady Giddy.

She had a good many *amourettes*, but she was on the whole discreet. She might possibly sin against every commandment in the decalogue,—

and probably did against one of them—but she was careful always to observe the greatest commandment of all "Thou shalt not be found out." Wives and mothers were inclined to be nasty now and then, but Lady Giddy held her own, and the world generally, and her world in particular, for the most part winked at her little affairs of the heart, and said "It was only that dear Lady Giddy's way."

Lady Giddy did not include Gwendolen in her house party, though Mrs. de Courcy Miles threw out some very strong hints indeed.

"After quartering herself and that girl upon us for the May-week last year, I call it most unfriendly," she said, forgetting that it was she who had worried Lady Giddy into staying with her. But Mrs. Miles was more than consoled by an invitation from Lord Baltinglass of Blarney, who, at Wilfrid's instigation, had taken a house at Wargrave for the Henley week.

Lady Giddy arranged a nice little party 'mixed and piquant' as they say of pickles. She invited Lady Elizabeth and Theodora, Lord Pimlico, Gaverigan, Colonel Lockhart, Miss Connecticut and Miss Mudlark, Sir Lauder Forbes, Lady Greyheather, and Miss Miller, Williams and Wilmot, and last but not least Violet Tresillian and Coryton. Lady Giddy was very proud of Violet in a way. She had done her much credit, for she was universally admitted to be one of the prettiest girls of last season.

Violet's wit, her beauty, heightened by her admirable taste in dress and her vague reputation of being an heiress had made her a centre of attraction. It was remarkable under the circumstances that she kept her faith with Coryton. She was just that sort of girl who might make a brilliant match in time; but somehow no very eligible *parti* came in her way throughout the season, at least not in the way of business —men often admire most

the women they would care to marry least—and
Coryton exercised an attraction,—it might almost
be called a fascination—over her, and besides she
was completely deceived as to his real financial
position.

Coryton accepted Lady Giddy's invitation gladly,
though he could only spare a few days. Parliament was still sitting, but Lord Southwark had
not much for him to do just now. By and by
would come that rush of bills which are always
hustled up to the Upper House at the fag end of
the Session. In the meantime the Lords were
waiting for work while the Commons were wrang-
ling. So Lord Southwark went off to his place
in Loamshire for a day or two, and his private
secretary ran down to Henley.

Without being head over ears in love with
Violet, Coryton liked to be with her, and was
anxious to urge his suit. He knew how volatile
she was and feared that she might throw him over

if someone, whom she considered a better match, presented himself. That would upset his calculations considerably, for was not Violet's dowry to pay his bills, his Election expenses and many other little luxuries? Therefore he was anxious to settle the matter without delay. Some awkward questions might turn up over the settlements, perhaps, but he thought he knew a way of evading them so far as he was concerned. He was quite ready to settle anything on Violet—on paper. When it came to paying over the money, Violet would be tied to him irrevocably.

"And she will be shrewd enough to accept the inevitable," he thought. "The real bond of wedlock is self-interest. Passion dies, love passes, but that remains. It is the motive power of most marriages, it is the secret of the endurance of them all."

Lady Giddy having arranged her little party, prepared to enjoy herself.

"You will have a good many boys among your guests," remarked Lady Elizabeth discontentedly to Lady Giddy, the afternoon of her arrival.

She and Theodora had come down by an early train. The others were not expected until just before dinner. Tea was over and Theodora had gone off—to have a 'look in', as she phrased it— at the stables. The two were sitting under the great elm-trees on the lawn. Her hostess had been running off her list for the benefit of Lady Elizabeth.

"I love boys," gushed Lady Giddy, a somewhat unnecessary statement her listener thought. "They take one so seriously, and do you know?—it is quite a pleasure to be taken seriously sometimes. It almost makes one believe in oneself."

"Which self?" asked Lady Elizabeth. "We all of us have three selves, the one we think we are, the one other people think we are, and the one we really are. Which self?"

"Oh, I don't know!" rejoined Lady Giddy indifferently, looking beyond her at the broad, flowing river, "the one people think we are, I suppose. It is refreshing to be believed in now and then, anyway."

Lady Elizabeth laughed amusedly.

"My good Gerty," she exclaimed. "You are getting quite sentimental. But tell me how comes it that the Baltinglasses are not included in your list? I thought you were such great friends."

"They have taken a house at Wargrave, a mile or so from here, or I should certainly have asked Wilfrid."

"Another boy!" said Lady Elizabeth. "He is a great friend of that new man one meets everywhere, Southwark's secretary, isn't he? They always seem to run in couples. Tell me, do you know anything about the girl Wilfrid is marrying. I saw her one day at Hurlingham—and I believe—I don't remember—she was at Blarney. She struck me as quite pretty. Who is she?"

" Oh nobody," rejoined Lady Giddy. " Quite a middle-class person, I assure you, the daughter of a Cambridge tutor or professor or something of the kind. Yes, she is pretty in a way, but utterly *gauche* and with no pretension to smartness."

" But you went to stay with the middle-class person at Cambridge last year, didn't you?" asked Lady Elizabeth, a trifle maliciously.

" Yes," said Lady Giddy composedly, " I was pestered into it. I know the girl's aunt a little, a terrible woman"—so do we speak of our dear friends—" whom I met in India long ago. We were at Simla one year together, and at Simla one gets to know all sorts of queer creatures, you know."

" Yes," said Lady Elizabeth, " quite so." She had heard a little of Lady Giddy's Simla experiences from another quarter. " Ah, here comes Theodora—Well, Theo, what do you think of the stables?"

"Rippin'," ejaculated Theodora. She was in the habit of clipping her g's; and her English—to put it mildly—was somewhat loose. "That's a gay little cob you've got, Gerty. I like him better than that fiddle-headed chestnut you rode last season."

"Yes," said Lady Giddy, falling into the same vernacular, "the chestnut was a bit nappy on the road, but fit as a flea when it came to going across country. I'm glad you like the cob, Theo, he's a gay little beast."

"I should like a mount on him to-morrow mornin', then I could tell better what he's made of, don't you know," said Theodora, decapitating a daisy with her stick.

"I don't see how you'll manage it," rejoined her hostess, "unless you turn out before breakfast. We'll have to go to the Regatta some time before luncheon."

"All right," said Theodora, "I'm game. I'll see

if I can't rout up Pim and we'll go for a spin together. It'll do him good; he's been gettin' very
slack lately and puttin' on weight in a manner that
is quite alarmin'."

Pimlico, however, (to whom she confided the
idea later on in the evening,) didn't seem to see
it, and so the ride was postponed for another day.

The next morning they all drove over in a big
brake to the Regatta—all, that is to say, except a
few of the more enthusiastic spirits, who preferred
to go by the river. But Lady Giddy and the bulk
of her party liked to take their pleasures easily.
So they drove over to Phyllis Court not too early
in the forenoon, and lunched comfortably under
some spreading trees in the grounds, and then joined
the privileged few who witness the Regatta from
Phyllis Court lawn, which slopes down to the
river's edge and commands an unrivalled view of
the scene of action. If any wished to go on the
river it was easy to get a boat from there.

It is needless to enter upon a detailed description of the Regatta. It may be taken for granted
that everyone has seen it. And this particular
Regatta was just the same as all the rest. There
were races going on presumably, though most of
the people did not seem to know much about
them ; there was the huge flotilla of boats of every
imaginable sort and shape, from the flower-
bedecked house-boat to the Canadian canoe. There
were nigger minstrels and comic singers, there
was the gay animated crowd on the river 'and on
the banks. Except that there was plenty of sun-
shine, and no rain—and it generally does rain for
Henley—there was nothing to mark out this Regatta
from those which had preceded it.

When Lady Giddy had disposed of her guests—
or rather when they had disposed of themselves,
as people have a knack of doing on these occasions—she looked around for Coryton, but learned
that he had gone off on the river with Violet.   A

faint sense of disappointment came over her. He amused her, and she had quite looked forward to a little flirtation with him.

She crossed the meadow with the intention of giving some directions to her servants, who were packing up the luncheon baskets, when suddenly she came upon someone with his hands clasped behind his head, reclining at full length under a chestnut tree. A cigarette was between his lips, and he was lazily watching the rings of blue smoke curl upwards in the summer air. In the distance Lady Giddy could see nothing but what seemed to her a heap of white flannels, with a straw hat alongside, but as she came nearer the heap resolved itself into shape, and she saw that it was Gaverigan.

"Upon my word," she exclaimed in a tone of laughing remonstrance, "this is really too bad of you, Harold. Quite apart from the ill compliment you pay me, what is the good of coming to the Regatta if you ostentatiously turn your back upon it?"

He sprang to his feet at the sound of her voice, and faced her with a smile.

"The Regatta!" he echoed, "I did not come to see the Regatta—that Cockney Carnival, that Paradise of Bohemia—but to see you," he added audaciously.

"You have a queer way of letting me know it," she rejoined coquettishly, "going apart by yourself in this manner—Well, I will not interrupt your meditations."

He laid a detaining hand on her arm, and looked pleadingly into her eyes.

"Do not be angry with me," he said contritely, "and do not go. Stay here with me. Surely it is better here than in yonder crowd?"

Lady Giddy thought so too. He was a handsome boy, quite as amusing as Coryton, she thought resentfully, though in a different way, and very much more in earnest. So they sat down and chatted on under the shady trees the whole of

the afternoon, while the band in the Isthmian
enclosure played its melodies, mellowed to them
by the distance. and the crowd on the river seemed
very far off. . . . .

"Gerty! Gerty!" cried a well-known voice at
last. "Ah, here you are. I have been looking
for you everywhere."

And Lady Elizabeth bore down upon them, a
little flushed with walking and considerably out of
temper.

"Nearly everyone is going into the house for
tea," she exclaimed in an injured tone. "Are you
coming? I don't like to go by myself, I don't know
the people."

"Dear me," apologized Lady Giddy, "I had no
idea it was so late, and I thought you were with
Lord Pimlico looking at the races."

"He's gone off with Theo somewhere. They've
been away together all the afternoon. As for the
races," continued Lady Elizabeth discontentedly,

as they walked towards the house, "I saw nothing
of them, I'm too old to care about such things,
and there are really very few people here one
knows. I only saw that terrible Sir Cincinnatus —
just in time, fortunately, to avoid him. If it hadn't
been for some queer actress creatures in a gaudy
house-boat and those delightful nigger minstrels,
I should have been bored to death. There was
really no one to talk to," she grumbled, determined to make her hostess feel the full enormity
of her delinquencies.

Meanwhile Coryton and Violet had paddled over
to Lord Muskery's launch in a Canadian canoe;
or rather Violet had done the paddling, while he
lay among the cushions and looked at her admiringly.
She appealed to his sense of fitness; there was a
vitality, a capability about her every movement.

Violet showed to advantage on the river. She
was not one of the women who dress overmuch
for Henley, but there was an exquisite freshness

and neatness about her well-fitting white serge, her
brown leather boots and the little hat with the dark
blue ribbon perched so coquettishly on her dainty
curls, which put to shame the more elaborate toilets
around her.

They fell to talking in a desultory way about
the subject which interested them most, namely
themselves. What would have struck a listener
most was the absence of sentiment on both sides.
There were no 'pawings and maulings,' no eloquent
looks, no half murmured words. They might have
been arranging their dinner instead of the great
event of their lives.

Nothing could be more admirable than their plans,
if only one fatal flaw had not run through them
all. Neither of them was frank with the other.
Coryton had urged in the most convincing way
the futility of a long engagement—the thought of
his unpaid bills had added a touch of eloquence to
his pleading—and Violet was a little tired of an

unsettled life, and of staying about with people whose only thought was to get her settled.

So they agreed to be married in the autumn.

Violet deftly piloted the canoe through the crowd of boats, until they came alongside Lord Baltinglass's launch—a luxurious craft with a gaily striped awning and heaps of cushions and flowers. Tea was going on when they boarded her, and there were a good many people sitting about, but the two whom they had come especially to see, Wilfrid and Gwendolen, were not there.

" They disappeared just after luncheon, and we have not seen them since," explained Mrs. de Courcy Miles, who wore a gorgeous costume, which she fondly imagined was just suited for the river, and which she had donned with a view of subjugating Lord Baltinglass of Blarney.

" We'll wait a little, they'll probably turn up for some tea presently," said Coryton.

" I don't know," ejaculated Miss Tyrconnel with

a pensive shake of her ringlets. "They have most likely forgotten all about it. Ah me! How sweet is Love's young dream! You can sympathize with them, can't you, dear?" And she looked towards Violet.

"I confess I can't," rejoined that young lady. "I don't understand that sort of thing myself. Give me one of those little cakes, Poley."

Miss Tyrconnel was right. Those of whom they were speaking had no more thought of tea than of the deluge. They were finding their all in one another.

Tyrconnel had sculled up the stream, and when they had got beyond sight of the shouting crowd he had moored the boat alongside the bank. Here, beneath the shade of a great alder-tree, whose branches swung their creamy blossoms low above heads, they whiled away the hours, 'the world forgetting, by the world forgot.'

They were both very much in love, though in a different way. Tyrconnel worshipped Gwendolen with all the passion of an emotional, impressionable nature. Passion seemed hardly the word to apply to Gwendolen. She was as pure as snow, and as cold. Yet the love she felt for him softened her nature somewhat, for she loved him with all the first freshness of a woman, who loves once and can never love again. But though it softened her, it did not change her. She strove to raise him to her pedestal, but she did not come down one step to meet him.

There are some women who love the part of counsellor and adviser. Gwendolen was one of these. She spoke to him eloquently of the iniquity of yielding to temptation,—she who had never known what it was to be tempted! She spoke to him of the sufferings of others,—she who had never known what it was to suffer! She was burning with a desire to set the world right,—she who had no more idea of the world than an unborn babe!

But however unselfish one may be, however rigid in one's spotless purity—when one is young and when one loves, one is apt now and then to let other considerations slide, and to find the joy of loving enough.

Gwendolen felt this to a certain extent to-day as she talked with her lover under the blossoming alder boughs and looked at the scudding ripples on the river's breast. Not that they talked much, for when one loves most one says least. Yet ever and anon their thoughts found vent in words, as now—when she was telling him how she meant to help him in the new life which lay before them. There was a glow of enthusiasm lighting up her face, he seemed to catch the reflex of it.

" Dear one," he said presently. " Do you never think of yourself? "

" If one lives for oneself one lives for but a little

thing," she answered. "I live for you, Wilfrid. You are my other self."

"And you are my nobler one," he vowed, bending nearer to her. Then a shadow fell over his face. "Sometimes," he said, "it seems to me that our happiness is too bright to last. Will you love me always?"

"Always, always," she repeated, looking at him out of the steady depths of her calm beautiful eyes.

Foolish vow, which lovers always use. What does it mean but that two beings, essentially changeable, pledge themselves never to change?

"Can you doubt me, Wilfrid?"

"No," he said, "never that—I only doubt my worthiness . . . . . Swear to me, Gwen, that nothing shall part us—nothing—past, present, or to come."

She looked at him, a little startled by his earnestness. It was one of his moods, she thought; it would pass.

" Have I not told you I will love you always,"
she said softly. " What can part us? The past
is over and gone. You have told me all." He
shrank a little at this, but she did not notice
it. " The future lies with God. Surely the present
is enough. We have no secrets from each other,
you and I. Let us then be happy in the perfect
confidence which love brings."

" The perfect confidence which love brings," he
repeated; " and love is merciful and forgiving,
is it not?"

He paused for a moment and bowed his head.
A struggle was going on within him. He had not
told her all. The memory of a half-forgotten
sin rose before him . . . . . And she trusted him . . . . .
He shrank from polluting her pure ears by even
hinting at what was past. But she trusted
him . . . . . And then he knew not how she would
take it. What some would consider a mere boyish
indiscretion might seem to Gwendolen a mortal

sin. No, he could not run the risk of losing her . . . . . But she trusted him . . . . .

" Gwen," he said hoarsely, " what if I were to tell you something more,—something——"

What he meant to say was never uttered. At that moment a shout of noisy laughter, the splashing of oars broke upon their ears and a boat passed by them. There were four people in it— of the Cockney Bohemian type. Two men were rowing, a girl was steering and another girl was lying down in the bows. They were all in boisterously high spirits, the girl in the bows had a banjo and a gaudy Japanese umbrella.

" Look out, Sally," cried one of the men, " take care where you are going to, or we shall be into that boat in a jiff."

Tyrconnel looked up to ward off the threatened danger and, as he did so, his eyes met full those of the girl steering. A shock of surprise and disgust ran through him, the words he had been forming died away upon his lips. He felt like one who is suddenly confronted with the ghost of an unforgiven sin. Here was the sin incarnate in the form of Sally Popkins.

Sally was also taken aback for the moment, with surprise probably. But she recovered an instant later, and leaned forward with a sort of half smile of recognition. But seeing that Tyrconnel responded not, the bow was strangled in its birth and her smile changed to a melancholy reproachful gaze. She pulled the wrong rope— there came a volley of remonstrance—more laughter, and the boat swept on.

But Gwendolen had caught that look too.

"Who is that person who looked at you so strangely, Wilfrid?" she asked with a puzzled air, "such an extraordinary looking creature! Have you seen her before?"

"I—I—don't know," stammered Tyrconnel confusedly—"I believe so. Don't you think it is time we were getting back, Gwen?—What a nuisance, I have let my scull fall into the water!"

In the excitement of fishing it out again, Gwendolen forgot, for a time, the look she had noticed on the girl's face.

CHAPTER XI.

THE GRAFTING OF THE GREEN BAY TREE.

We mutually pledge to each other our lives
our fortunes and our sacred honour.
                    —THOMAS JEFFERSON.

THE Coryton-Tresillian wedding was pronounced
by the society papers to be one of the events
of the autumn.   That is to say, there were a
great many well-dressed people at Saint Peter's,
Eaton-square, with favours and flowers galore.
The bride's dress—like most bride's dresses—was
of ivory duchesse satin, trimmed with Alençon lace
and there were the usual sprigs of aphrodysiac
orange-blossom, inappropriate emblem of innocence.

There were eight white bridesmaids with Charles the First hats and long white feathers that waggled all down their backs; there were two little page-boys, nephews of Sir Edward Tresillian, who held up the bride's train and looked quite picturesque with their golden love-locks and cavalier costumes of white velvet.

After the ceremony, everybody trooped off to the Lockharts' house in Grosvenor-place, kindly lent for the occasion, and suggestive comments were interchanged, hollow congratulations offered. The wedding presents were displayed on long tables all round the drawing-room and suggested a charity bazaar, especially by their tawdriness and vulgarity. Lord Southwark had sent a half-guinea nickel ink-pot, which Violet mentally destined for the servants' hall, when she got one. Seventeen people of wealth and good position had sent silver muffineers, which afterwards only fetched two and threepence each as old silver. An obscure painter-man had taken this opportunity of exhibiting one of his daubs to a larger audience than he had ever secured before and an obscure novelist had taken the same opportunity of advertising his three-volume shocker. Miss Tyrconnel's present of half a dozen Nainsook night-caps was hidden away under the plethoric family Bible with which she accompanied them. Pimlico's roulette-board was carefully wrapped up in its cloth. Coryton and Violet were supposed to be rising stars and their most ephemeral acquaintances took the opportunity of proving their regard without overtaxing their pockets. Violet had remarked, as each fresh present arrived, that such meanness defeated itself, for the object of a wedding present was to give pleasure and exact remembrance, while these trumpery offerings did neither.

Violet had gone through the trying ordeal very well, contriving to combine a certain affectation of demureness and a pathetic by-play of her big

round eyes with an airy cheerfulness as rare in
a bride as it is delightful. The women congratu-
lated her ironically on her pluck and went off to
whisper in each other's long ears that it was
'most unmaidenly.' The men were inclined to
think Coryton had got 'rather a handful,' but all
agreed she was 'a deuced pretty girl.' A knot
of young men began discussing the question how
long she would take to get tired of him and how
she would treat her admirers in another six
months.

"They are neither of them the sort of people
one would care to marry," said Gaverigan airily.
"They are fairly good company so long as one
does not see too much of them. A week alone
with either would bore me off my head—to say
nothing of a lifetime! People who want to get
on in life always bore me. They are so cursed
commonplace."

"They are very cynical," said Toadey-Snaile,

who disliked Gaverigan, "and there is nothing so commonplace as that nowadays."

"What nonsense!" exclaimed Williams. "The girl's as fresh and original as they make them. I've heard her startle the stupidest people with the things she says——"

"Yes, I know she often startles you," sneered Wilmot, with the privileged rudeness of intimacy.

"Be quiet. I only mean she says astounding things to the most correct people and yet every man, woman, and child is devoted to her. I call that a proof of cleverness, if you like."

"How sick she'll get of Mr. Coryton before the honeymoon's over," put in Theodora, who always joined in the confabulations of young men. "I do hate young men who always let you see they are thinking about their prospects."

"'M yes. Other people's prospects don't interest one, do they?" said Gaverigan.

"That depends on who they are."

" Pim, for instance? "

" You cheeky chap! No, I only meant that it
offends me to have 'comin' men' give themselves
all those airs before they've come, don't you
know? Big bosses don't put on all that side. It's
all very well to say he's clever. I don't call it
clever to have that manner."

" Oh! well. I don't know. People generally
take one at one's own valuation. Don't you think
so, Corry? " Gaverigan went on, as the bridegroom
joined the group.

" Or at that of what the lawyers call one's
'next friend,' who knows more than all one's
weak points and—like the 'damned good-natured
fellow' he is—takes a pleasure in proclaiming
them."

" But surely frankness is one of the highest
privileges of intimacy."

" Frankness! What is that? " he replied, turning on his heel. " Frankness consists in telling

plausible untruths to your face, and outrageous ones behind your back, doesn't it? "

" Bridegroom seems fresh, don't he? " said Pimlico, in his sporting lingo. " Vixie'll have to ride him with the snaffle and put the blinkers on him."

At last Violet got a chance of saying a few words privately to her husband.

" For Heaven's sake let's get this over as soon as we can," she whispered. " I've thanked two hundred and ninety-three people for their congratulations and a hundred and seventy-five for their presents, without making a single mistake. Nineteen old men have said. ' God bless you!' to me, and at least as many old women have made the most embarrassing allusions."—She blushed in the daintiest way as she said this.—"And really I can't stand it much longer."

" There's only half an hour more, thank goodness! " returned Coryton, his dark face lighting up with a sunny smile. "I am afraid I have been quite rude to some of these precious sight-seers. Modern marriage is really a most disagreeable process. If we ever have to go through it again, we'll go straight from the church to the station, won't we?"

Violet laughed. "To judge from our impatience, anybody'd think we were madly in love with each other,—the sort of young fools who go in for 'love in a cottage,' don't you know?"

"Instead of a honeymoon at Monte Carlo, followed by love in a little box in Mayfair, eh?" he returned. "Well, even if I weren't yearning for heaven with you, I should be sick of this purgatory by this time."

"Come, you're getting on. Compliments from Poley are compliments indeed, aren't they, Miss Gargoyle?"

"Don't know. Never tried 'em," returned that young woman in her downright way. "S'pose you're off soon. Anyhow I am. This kind of

show sickens me.   No offence, mind.   I hope you'll
have a real good time.   Must say I envy you
Monte just now,—it's rippin' there before the rabble
sets in.   You and I must be good pals all the same,
although you have gone to stud.   I don't mind lettin'
you into a secret"—and she took Violet aside
mysteriously and talked to her in a loud stage
whisper—" Pim and I are going to follow suit
in the spring.   Ain't it horrid?   I blush all over
every time I think of it."

" You'll soon get used to it," laughed Violet,
not knowing what to make of all this unusual
amiability.   " Well, if you really must be going,
good-bye.   Thanks awfully for coming to see me
' go to stud,' as you call it.   I daresay we shall
see you down south later on."

The guests were thinning a little and it was
almost time to prepare for departure.   Violet heaved
a great sigh of relief.   She was not quite sure
she had done wisely in marrying this man and a

haunting dread of the future possessed her. She liked him and believed he was bound to get on. But that was very different from the love which hopeth all things, endureth all things,—even poverty in a cottage. She laughed softly to herself. Poverty! No, that was not a thing she could endure with anyone. Phew! Was she so very cocksure that there would be plenty to live on? The settlements had been very carelessly gone into and, when she came to think of it, the £1000 a year that had been settled on her had only been settled on paper and, for all she knew, her husband might not have a thousand pence to bless himself with. Her solicitors had not advised minute inquiries, as the object of their diplomacy was to conceal by vague promises and ambiguous phrases the nakedness of the land, and it was feared, as Mr. Soapsuds, the senior partner, phrased it, that 'inquiries might breed inquiries.'

However, she was not a person to anticipate

evil. So long as things were going well for the moment, she was quite content to let the future take care of itself. Poley was a dear boy and the beginning of one's first honeymoon is always an inspiring period even for the most *blasé*. She determined none the less to take an early opportunity of learning the exact state of affairs from her husband and putting an end to this suspense. Her reflections were cut short by the appearance of Wilfrid Tyrconnel with outstretched hand and beaming face.

"At last I have an opportunity of giving you all my good wishes!" he exclaimed breathlessly. "I have been looking for an opportunity all the afternoon, but you were always busy with some old fossil or other. And now you are just off and you will never be the same Vixie again."

"Bless me! Have you got such a volume of good wishes for me as all that? Very well, fire ahead. I can still give you ten minutes."

"Don't joke, Vixie. I am quite sad about it. Believe me," he stammered, "I do hope you'll be very, very happy. I used to think at one time I might perhaps have had some share in making you happy. But somehow we seem to have drifted apart. Corry's a good chap and all that, but somehow I never thought that he—that you——"

"Were likely to fall head over ears in love with anybody, least of all with each other," she said rather bitterly, helping him through in his confusion.

"Well, he has not your fine feelings. I never thought you were cut out for each other exactly. But as you have chosen him, I suppose you do love him and I hope and pray that he may make you happy—may be worthy of you."

"Pray!" she murmured, half to herself, with a shade of displeasure in her tones. Why did this youth come and put doubts into her head just as she was making an effort to put them out?

"Yes, *pray*," he returned earnestly. "You know I never set up to be a religious chap."—Violet smiled, as the thought of Gwendolen flitted through her mind.—"But I believe that sometimes prayers are heard and I, who have a very deep regard for you, do pray earnestly that all possible happiness may be yours."

He seemed deeply moved and Violet's quick sympathies were touched at once.

"You are a kind boy, Pidge," she said gently, taking his hand, "and I am sure I can always count on you as a friend, even though others may come between us."

A blush rose to his cheek.

"No one shall prevent my being your friend, *always*," he said simply.

"Gwendolen doesn't like me——" she began.

"You and she have never got on very well, because you are so different," he interrupted. "But you wrong her in saying she does not like you. She does not understand you as I do, but she is always eager to think the best of everyone. We shall always desire your welfare. You know," he added confusedly, " that we are going to be married almost immediately! "

" I have long expected it. I shall certainly— 'pray' for you ! Miss Haviland deserves all congratulations. Look here, Pidge, aren't you rather a queer fellow, coming here to declare your eternal devotion to me, just when I'm married to another man and you're engaged to another girl? All right, old boy," she added almost affectionately, " we'll swear eternal friendship, won't we ? I only hope you may be as happy as we are going to be. Eh, Poley?" she added, as her husband came to claim her.

What a relief when at last they were clear of the nagging crowd and were driving off to the station with tell-tale grains of rice in the folds

of their clothes and an old shoe lingering among
the rugs! For the first time there was a feeling
of constraint between them and neither spoke for
some time. At last Violet, whom a silence always
bored, put on a little sentimental pout and said,

"Are you quite sure you don't regret the step
we're taking, Poley?"

" Oh! yes," he said without enthusiasm. " We
thought it well out beforehand and it's going to
lead to a big boom,—all the bigger perhaps because
we are hampered by no childish illusions about
love."

Violet screwed up her face with a dissatisfied air.

" If you say so," she returned, " I suppose it
must be so. But I don't see the necessity of
repeating it so often. If you don't love me, you
might at least have the politeness to pretend to
on our wedding-day."

There was enough resentment in Violet's tones
to arrest Coryton's attention, but it never struck

him that it could be anything more than pique.
He was in a nervous irritable mood, chiefly from
a haunting doubt that perhaps this marriage was
a rash speculation, as well as from extreme anxiety
to know what they would have to live upon. He
was meditating how he should ask her, but even
his cynical nature shrank from such a step at
this stage of the honeymoon. Besides, his policy
of always⟩seeking to please and keep everybody
in perpetual good humour had become so much a
habit with him that it was almost a second nature.
So he took his cue from her mood at once and
patted her little gloved hand with some show of
tenderness, saying,

"I believe we love each other as far as we
are capable of such an emotion, either of us. At
any rate we have what is much more important
for a happy marriage, and that is, the same
interests and the same character."

Violet smiled rather sadly.

"I am foolish enough to care a great deal more for you than you do for me," she said, "and I know that any unhappiness the marriage may bring forth will fall upon my shoulders. Some people say it is always the woman that suffers most. I don't believe that. It is the one who feels most deeply."

"It is a mistake to feel deeply about anything," he said lightly, "and I don't believe we either of us really do. Least of all should we feel deeply during that mad carnival, known as the honeymoon. A well-arranged life is one continuous honeymoon and a well-arranged honeymoon has nothing of real life about it except its continuity."

"Those are good rules for fair weather. But there must be love to take one through a storm. If we were poor, for instance"—she scrutinized his face anxiously, as she said this, but learned nothing,—"if we were poor, we couldn't rub along on those terms."

"Or on any others, for the matter of that," he returned. "I don't agree with you that love would help to make poverty tolerable. One would feel so much more acutely the privations undergone by somebody one loved better than oneself,—if you can conceive the existence of such a person," he added, with his sneering smile.

"You rascal, of course I can," she answered reproachfully, "and I believe the pleasure of smoothing away those privations for him would more than counterbalance the pain of enduring them—or even of witnessing them."

"Come now, Vixie. Such a sentiment from you is too outrageous. You really might give up trying to astonish me now. I believe you only say things just to see how wide you can make people open their eyes."

"Well, that *is* an amusement, as you know yourself. But I am serious this time. I believe—quite apart from sentiment or any such rot—that love is a most useful commodity in marriage,—if you can get it."

"I daresay. But you can't. There isn't such a thing, at least not after the first month is over and the gilt has been rubbed off the gingerbread."

"At any rate love is the only thing that can make poverty endurable."

"I don't agree at all. Love is excess of sentiment. If poverty could ever be made endurable, it would be by the utter absence of sentiment. I have always tried to educate myself not to care a twopenny damn what happens. That is the true philosophy. If you have that and an unshakable belief in yourself, nothing can disconcert you. Poverty will only be a temporary inconvenience, hardship a means to an end, and economy a policy."

"What a subject for a honeymoon! I am sure I hope we may never have to put our theories to the proof. As for me, I have no patience with poor

people. It is always people's own fault if they
are poor. If you play your cards well, you can
always get credit for your luxuries and then the
necessaries can take care of themselves. And the
people I have least patience with are those who are
for ever parading their poverty. I consider that
much more vulgar than parading riches, as Lord
Baltinglass and people of his kidney do. However
poor I was, I should have too much self-respect
to parade my poverty."

"Of course, no wise person parades poverty,
unless he is very rich, any more than a true gentleman ever makes a parade of riches unless he
is as poor as a rat. Then he has to."

By this time they had reached the station and
they found they had some minutes to wait before
the train, which was to take them as far as Dover.
Sir Edward Tresillian's confidential valet had made
all the arrangements for comfort and privacy,
which a honeymoon is supposed to require. A

private compartment had been taken, and the usual necessaries of travel provided: a hamper from Benoist's, all the evening papers and a selection of two-shilling novels.

Couples on their honeymoons are supposed not to want companionship. At any rate they feel they must conform to custom so far as to travel by themselves. People always look at the newly-married in a horribly embarrassing way and modesty, as well as custom, requires a retreat. But when the retreat has been found and the guard has tipped his last wink and the engine has given its first outward puff, food and literature are invaluable resources.

"How thoughtful of Cribble to get us all those yellow-backs," Violet exclaimed, as soon as they were installed. "I really could not have stood another half hour of your epigrams."

"Well, there's Gaverigan coming along with luggage and hampers and an air of infinite content on his face. Would you like him in our carriage to relieve you of the tedium of my society all the way to Dover?"

Nothing that anyone could say ever ruffled Coryton's imperturbable good humour.

"Oh! yes," Violet exclaimed, clapping her hands delightedly. And then, seeing a comical look of distress on her husband's face, she added, "Not that I don't like being with you, Poley, old boy, but we shall see such a lot of each other presently that an hour or two now won't make any difference."

"Don't distress yourself, Vixie," he said, as he beckoned Gaverigan. "I'm not so thin-skinned as all that."

Gaverigan was on his way to Monte Carlo and was at once subjected to a good deal of chaff about his discretion in concealing his intention at the wedding. He vowed that he never made up his mind to go there until the last moment and always kept the whole thing a profound secret.

In this case he had been especially deterred from a confession by his desire not to intrude upon the happy pair, when they would most of all wish to be left alone.

The happy pair, however, protested that that was what they least of all wished.

"You can't think how shy we are, Mr. Gaverigan," Violet exclaimed. "Do come and be chaperon."

Gaverigan, however, required a great deal of persuasion, but was at last sufficiently tickled by the novelty of the proposal made him to give way. They had a very merry journey down, the hampers occupying them most of the way and a game of studpoker keeping them amused for the rest.

"Well, I'm sure this is the most original journey I ever heard of," Gaverigan exclaimed more than once. "I can only think of one detail that could possibly have made it more original and that would have been for Coryton to travel in the public car and for you and me to go alone in the honeymoon compartment, eh, Vixie?"

"I wish we'd thought of that," she laughed, "and so does Poley. He's tired of me already."

Coryton certainly looked as if the whole business bored him. He was feeling uneasy about the future,—an unusual thing with him—and his nervousness seemed to communicate itself to his wife. Her last remark was uttered with a good deal of feeling, which the bantering tone she had assumed did not entirely cloak. Coryton, who had quick perceptions, noticed it at once and watched her curiously for some moments.

Then he turned to Gaverigan with a ludicrous shrug and said,

"You see, we're so confoundedly shy about all this business that we have to make a parade of indifference before other people, but when we are alone, we're just as much spoons as any other honeymooners, aren't we, Vixie?"

" This is the most agreeable journey I've ever known," exclaimed Gaverigan, interrupting him,—" and the journey from London to Monte Carlo always is very agreeable,—at any rate to an expert traveller."

' Like yourself," Violet put in.

Gaverigan made a deep bow.

" I say," he went on, " it would be jolly if you people would consent to come straight on, instead of stopping at Dover. It would be so delightfully unconventional and we'd be as happy as sandboys. The journey is infinitely pleasanter if you do it without stopping. You'll have plenty of time to register your luggage again at Dover and send a wire to the Lord Warden. I've secured a cabin for the boat, which is very much at your service."

" I hate travelling at night," said Violet hastily. " Besides, there are limits even to unconventionality."

She turned appealingly to her husband, who was watching her with a comical expression.

"Certainly, my dear, very distinct limits," he replied. "In fact, I always say that people only seek to attract attention by being unconventional when they can't do it in any other way. There's one for you, old boy," he added, getting up and slapping Gaverigan on the shoulder, as the train rattled into Dover-Town station.

"But we shall meet out there very soon, Mr. Gaverigan," Violet added, her face brightening up with pleasure at the prospect of arrival. "We shall spend a fortnight or so in Paris and then go on south by easy stages. I am counting on you to initiate me into all the mysteries of roulette. I suppose everybody will be there,—Lady Giddy and the Pigeon and the rest. I mean to have a regular good time."

Gaverigan bade her good-bye with more effusion than that *nil admirari* youth usually thought it incumbent on himself to display. Violet's character interested him, and he had often contemplated the

possibility of making love to her. As to the
wisdom of her wedding with Coryton, he had been
in considerable doubt all along.

" Poor little girl," he murmured thoughtfully,
as the train went on towards the pier. " I'm
afraid she'll have rather a rough time of it with
that great, cold, unemotional fathead, Coryton. I
shouldn't think anything would move him, either
tears, or appeals, or death itself. So long as
everything goes smoothly he'll be smooth and fair,
and even charming in his way. But directly anything goes wrong, there'll be the very devil.
They are both clever and, with a fair amount of
luck, there is no reason why they shouldn't make
a boom of life. But they can't either of them
have much money behind them and, without that,
it's always an up-hill game . . . . She is much fonder
of him than he is of her. But that'll wear off.
It's always so to begin with . . . . . I suppose they'll
drift into being knights of industry one way or

another. But I hope not. She's much too nice
for that sort of thing.... I should like to meet
her again when she's lost her illusions,—if she
has ever had any....! Here, porter, take all
these things on board the Calais boat."

CHAPTER XII.

THE LORD WARDEN.

Philosophy triumphs easily over past and future
evils, but present evils triumph over philosophy.
—La Rochefoucauld.

A cosy sitting-room with a fire and a tempting
dinner awaited the Corytons at the Lord Warden
hotel, but not much appetite remained to either
of them after the anxieties of the day and the
convivial journey down. Violet heaved a deep
sigh of content as she flung off her wraps and
drew up an arm-chair to the fire. She looked
very picturesque with the glow of the flames
lighting up her face and there was a look of

happiness upon it which few had ever been privileged to see there.

"Dear, dear Poley!" she exclaimed with some feeling, as soon as they were alone, "I really believe I must be in love with you. I feel in such an ecstatic condition, as if some good fairy had suddenly granted me all my desires and I had nothing left to wish for. I thought that journey would never come to an end, but now my happiness makes up for all that went before. Oh! Poley, tell me I'm not dreaming. Really it seems almost too good to be true."

He bent down and kissed her forehead without enthusiasm.

"It is quite true, nevertheless," he said half absently, "and I'm sure I hope you'll go on being happy. I mean to. But what has come over you, Vixie? I thought you professed not to care a snap about anything or anybody."

"You know I care about you," she answered softly.

"Oh! yes, we are very good friends." he returned discontentedly, "but we never laid claim to a grand passion, did we? Our marriage was one of interest quite as much as of friendship after all."

"Oh! Poley," she said reproachfully.

"Well, what is it you're grumbling at? Have you ever taken any other tone towards it yourself?"

"One may not have illusions, but surely it is not necessary to go on rubbing in that or any other unpleasant truth. I think at any rate on our wedding night you might have the grace to pretend you care for me, even if you don't."

"Don't let's quarrel, Vixie, especially about trifles. We ought to understand each other by this time. We have the same interests and are going, each of us, to do our utmost to further them. What truer love can there be than that? Is it not much more practical as well as much more lasting than the mawkish thing that poets and children drivel about?"

Violet's brow had clouded over and she was looking, rather dismally, straight into the fire.

"I hardly think either of us would care about love in a cottage!" he went on obstinately; "and, after all, poverty is the only test of absolutely disinterested affection."

"I don't know why you persist in talking about that," she remonstrated, "as we are not going to be put to that test, it would surely be more gallant to assume that we should weather it."

"I am very glad to hear you say that," he replied, seizing the opportunity he had been leading up to, "for do you know, I have been rather anxious about our money prospects all through."

Violet looked at him in amazement for some minutes without speaking.

"What on earth do you mean?" she asked at last, without a trace of sentiment left in her voice.

"What you've settled on me is alone more than enough to keep the wolf from the door, and I imagine it isn't the whole of your income."

He paced up and down the room several times in an agitated way and then stood facing her with his hands by his side, clenched in a somewhat theatrical attitude. She looked up at him, shading her face from the firelight, and noticed that he had turned a ghastly pale and was breathing hard and fast.

"Don't stand there in that Adelphi attitude, but tell me the truth," she said coldly. "It's too late now for it to make any difference."

"The truth is," he said hoarsely, "that I haven't any income at all. I have been living on my capital for some years and now there is precious little even of that left."

"There are my settlements at any rate," she returned. It was meant for an assertion, but her voice sounded rather like a trembling interrogative.

" Settlements—bah!   They were only on paper."

" And do you—mean—to—tell—me—?" she faltered.

" That we have only your income and a hundred or so between us and starvation?   Precisely."

"Well, but I haven't any income either," she blurted out, quite taken aback.

There was a long silence before either of them spoke again.   Like the hard-swearing farmer in the anecdote, they thought that no words of theirs were 'equal to the occasion.'   Coryton had often contemplated the possibility of such a catastrophe, but in his heart of hearts he had never believed in it and now that it had come upon him, it was as overwhelming as a bolt from the blue.   He was of an extraordinarily sanguine temperament and, as everything had always gone well with him during his life, he was firmly convinced that it always would.   Failure is never so intolerable as when success has become habit.   With Coryton a belief in his good star was almost a second nature and the shock of his first failure seemed utterly to unnerve him. It was as if somebody had suddenly dealt him a blow full in the face and he had no means of returning it. He stood beside a stiff velvet chair, pale and drawn, his hands twitching nervously. It was impossible to slap fortune back again, so he could only turn his resentment against his wife.

She was, however, the first to break the silence. It was in a very low voice, rather sad than reproachful, that she asked,

"What could have made you do it? You might have known I hadn't much money and you never pretended you loved me."

He had drawn aside the curtain and was looking out into the dismal road, badly lighted and now almost deserted, biting his lips and trying not to think. He heard what she said, but gave no sign that he had done so.

"And I thought you were so clever," she went on, her irritation increasing with his show of indifference, "that you were going to be such a success. But it turns out you are no better than a fool. Fool! Fool! Fool!" she repeated, raising her voice angrily.

He turned half round and cast a contemptuous glance at her.

"I might say the same to you," he answered with a sneer.

"I never deceived you about it," she retorted hotly. "You could have found out exactly how much I had got, for the asking. But you deceived me, you deceived my uncle, you even deceived the solicitor."

"That at least was clever," he said sarcastically, turning his back and looking out of the window · again.

"Clever!" she almost shouted. "If that's being clever, give me a born idiot. Anybody can take people in, if he chooses to tell lies. And you weren't content with telling lies,—you stooped to draw up sham settlements not worth the paper they were written on. I call it fraud. It was obtaining something by false pretences. I believe you could be locked up for it, just as much as if you'd cheated people with a sham cheque. Clever indeed! What could have been your object in behaving like such a silly fool? You've succeeded in ruining your own prospects as well as mine. What could have possessed you? "

She was working herself up into a passion as she went on and the last sentence was jerked out with an emphasis that was almost fury.

Coryton watched her, as one might watch a drama, and there was a touch of admiration in his gaze. She looked very fine in her rage. She had risen as she spoke and was facing him, erect and defiant.

" What possessed me ? " he repeated. " I suppose

it was the idea that you had cleverness and money enough for both of us."

"Money!" she cried, with all that contempt for the precious metals, which only those, who have never had the handling of them, know how to express. "So that was your object in marrying me! Well then, all I have to say is that you've made a great mistake."

After a pause she added, "A fatal mistake for both of us. You don't seem to think anything of the opportunities I have lost through my folly in trusting you. I might have married a dozen men just as clever and far more honourable than you. A nice position you have brought me to, tied for life to a creature I hate and despise and with scarcely a penny to bless himself. The only course I can see open to me is to apply for a divorce and go and live abroad."

"I am afraid the judges would scarcely satisfy you in that way yet," he replied with an acid smile.

' Well, then, I shall leave you and you can apply for it or not as you think fit. I am not going to live any more with a scoundrelly broken-down adventurer, who hasn't even the wit to cheat cleverly."

" It's no use losing your temper," returned Coryton with an imperfect effort to appear calm. " Everything you say applies equally, indeed doubly to you. A man has no means of finding out what income a girl has before he marries her. It would be considered indelicate if he even hinted that he wanted to know. A girl on the other hand is generally safeguarded by relations and lawyers and people and it is her fault—or at any rate theirs—if she doesn't get all she needs settled on her."

' It was precisely over the settlements that you cheated us."

" Yes, but do you suppose for an instant that a parcel of crafty, worldly old lawyers would have let you be cheated, if they hadn't had orders to get you off at any cost? If there has been any sharp practice in this matter, I certainly think I have been more sinned against than sinning."

Violet made an impatient gesture, as if about to speak.

"It is no use indulging in heroics," he said in deliberate tones; "we have got to think out what we'll do. I admit it is serious enough, but we shall gain nothing by acting rashly on the impulse of the moment. I will go downstairs and think the situation over. Perhaps you may be in a calmer state of mind to-morrow morning."

He advanced to kiss her, having now quite recovered his cold imperturbable manner, but she waved him back imperially.

"Don't touch me!" she cried, "don't dare to touch me, you miserable idiot. Out of my sight and may I never set eyes on you again."

Coryton knitted his brows and was on the point of making an angry retort, but he abruptly changed his mind and, taking up his hat and stick, left the room without a word. As he passed out of the hotel he said to the porter in cold matter-of-fact tones,

"Mrs. Coryton is unwell. You will give orders that a bedroom may be got ready for me on the same floor as hers."

"Lor'," exclaimed the porter confidentially to the barmaid, when Coryton had gone out. "that only shows yer 'ow deceptive appearances is. I could 'ave sworn they was a nooly-married couple, and ye know I 'ave 'ad some experience of married couples in moy toime."

"I never thought as they was," returned the barmaid with a toss of the head over her superior astuteness. "Their things was noo an' all that, but there was none of the billin' and cooin' ye sees in them 'oneymooners. Prob'bly they ain't used ter travellin' an' 'ad ter git a noo rig out."

"Billin' an' cooin' don't prove nothink," said

the porter, indignant at the doubts cast upon his experience. " Why, Lor' bless yer, 'arf of them toffs just marry for what they can git an' there ain't no more love about their marriages than there is rabbit in one of our rabbit poys. 'Twon't be so when you an' oi gits spliced, will it, Mariar?" he added with a leer.

" Oh! go on wi' yer, Mr. Briggs, I ain't so much as promised as we ever shall," she replied with one of those grotesque attempts at coquetry in which the British middle and lower classes always fail so signally.

Meanwhile Coryton was making his way to the pier in a very gloomy frame of mind. It was a bad business certainly, but he was of a sanguine temperament and nothing ever affected him seriously for long.

If they had not money, they had brains, which was much better, he tried to argue to himself. But the consolation to be found in that reflection

was distinctly forced and he found it more difficult
to take a hopeful view than he had ever done
before.   He still believed in his destiny, of course,
and he still believed in his wife's, but he foresaw
months and even years of struggles and was not
by any means sure that either would be able to
stand them.   His was not a demonstrative nature,
but his regard for Violet was none the less sincere.
They had always been good friends, he reflected,
and there was no reason why they should not
continue to be so.   If only they had found out the
true state of each other's affairs four and twenty
hours before, they might each have carved out a
great career and enjoyed many opportunities of
doing good turns to each other.

Now they were a mutual handicap, chronic obsta-
cles in the path of success.   Their position was a
standing refutation of the silly proverb about
union being strength.   If only the fatal step of
that afternoon could be retraced now, before the girl

was compromised. A foolish scheme passed through his head for a collusive divorce or nullity suit, but he speedily dismissed the idea, not so much for its difficulty as for the scandal it would create. The slightest scandal in a public man's private life is nowadays made much more of than any public enormity he may have been guilty of, however outrageous.

There was no getting over hard facts. Too much astuteness had brought him to grief. He saw the folly of it all now that it was too late and he was not long in coming to the conclusion that his only course was to make the best of a bad job. But that did not make the bad job any more acceptable. The blow to his vanity was the hardest part of all and he walked up and down the pier, reproaching himself in as unmeasured terms as any Violet had made use of towards him.

The charm of Coryton's character was that nothing ever really upset him for long. Before he had been out an hour the worst of his fit of the blues was over and, as he stopped to light a cigar, the match revealed a fairly cheerful face, in which no trace of his worries remained.

"After all," he concluded, as he turned his steps back to the hotel, "the thing to be thought of is the future, not the past. I daresay our marriage will not turn out any the less satisfactory for the queer way in which the honeymoon has begun."

Violet meanwhile was taking the matter far more to heart. Her husband's indifference had revealed to her a fact which she had long suspected, that she was really and truly in love with him. When this first occurred to her, she had scouted it with a merry laugh. That she, who had never taken anything or anybody seriously—scarcely even herself—should fall in love, was too preposterous a notion.

For a long time she had kept up the pretence that her marriage with Coryton was to be merely one of convenience—the alliance of two clever people for their mutual advancement—and when she had detected the first symptoms of love-sickness, she was utterly puzzled and thought of sending for the doctor to prescribe for influenza.

As the symptoms became unmistakable, she became even more moody and fitful than young ladies usually are during this distemper. Still she did not give up the attempt to deceive herself on the subject until after the marriage, when she was stung to the quick by the complacent way, in which he took it for granted that love was an impossibility between them.

Her heart now sank within her and she felt a strange disappointed yearning, which could leave no further room for doubt. It was this aching of unsatisfied love, far more than the revelation of mere money trouble, that kept her tossing and moaning, in agony of mind, all through her wedding night. Unrequited love is hard enough for any woman to bear, but it becomes almost unendurable when united with pride and cleverness and unscrupulousness sufficient to remove mountains.

The revelation of her husband's poverty had strengthened rather than diminished Violet's love for him. She felt that even love in a cottage would be endurable with him; that there would be an infinite joy in denying herself pleasures and luxuries in order that he might enjoy them in her stead; that their temporary poverty—for, of course, with such a genius as her husband, poverty could only be temporary—would aid her in winning his love.

But her heart sank as she contemplated the immediate future. She was not used to poverty and, from all accounts, it seemed to be unanimously considered a very disagreeable thing. Poverty would leave her so desperately alone in the world. There are none so desperately alone as the poor rich. The rich poor are happy : their wants are few, luxury is undreamed of and they can save money on a hundred a year. The poor rich, on the other hand, have appearances to keep up, expensive tastes, which grudge if they be not satisfied, and expensive friends, with whom friendship means the exaction of usefulness. Violet knew full well that, if she and her husband could not manage to keep up appearances, they would speedily be dropped by all their fairweather friends, who now only saluted what they believed to be the rising sun. And what more utter loneliness was imaginable than the solitary society of an unsympathetic husband ?

It was over some such thoughts as these that Violet fell into a heavy slumber in the small hours of the morning.

When she awoke, Coryton was standing beside her with a tea-tray and her pleasure at his thoughtfulness overcame all recollection of last night's disagreeable scene.

"This is good of you, Poley," she said, with a grateful look in her tear-stained eyes.

The traces of her weeping and the anxiety tinged with affection in her tones could not but affect Coryton, nor could he ignore her undeniable prettiness in her nightdress of lace and silk, with the rosy light through the blind tinting the rounded outline of her face. He felt almost remorseful and answered her with far more deference than was usual with him.

"Not at all. I only came to see if you were inclined to come on to Paris by the early boat. We shall be as cross as two sticks in this dead-alive place. At Paris we can at least get something fit to eat and see a naughty play—two admirable specifics against the blues."

Violet brightened up at once.

"You have forgiven me for my crossness last night?" she asked eagerly. "You know I didn't mean a word I said."

" Well, don't let it occur again," he returned
half playfully, in the tone of one lecturing a naughty
child. " We've got an up-hill struggle before us—
the struggle of keeping up appearances on nothing.
But that is the very reason why we should try
to pull together all the more harmoniously in
harness. We are in for it now and we can't afford
to quarrel. If any people ever were necessary to
each other, it's you and I. Now get your things
together as quickly as you can and we'll have a
week's dissipation in Paris. By the end of it we shall
probably see our way more clearly. There is no
such aid to reflection as a good bout of dissipation."

" We shall get on all right," replied Violet,
whose good humour had now entirely returned,
" if only you've a little patience with me. To-
night we'll dine at the Café Riche, take a *baignoire*
at the Variétés and wind up with the Moulin
Rouge. I have always wanted to be taken to the
Moulin Rouge."

" All right," he assented smiling, " but you must be ready to start in half an hour."

Thus melted the first and last cloud that overshadowed the blossoming of the Green Bay Tree.

CHAPTER XIII.

THE RIFT WITHIN THE LUTE.

Too fair to worship, too divine to love.
—H. H. MILMAN.

CANNES is decidedly the pleasantest place on the Riviera for those who are admitted to the vulgar and inflated clique, which passes there for Society. It is a close oligarchy which makes up for its vulgarity by an affectation of exclusiveness.

Monte Carlo, on the other hand, is as much a democracy as a great public-school, where neither rank nor brains nor culture are the passport to respect, but only success at games.

Physical-force games are the school idols, games of pure chance those of Monte Carlo, and the worshippers are on a footing of such absolute equality as is only found in the dreams of crack-brained political philosophers.   Nowhere else in the whole round world will you find duchesses of the blood and horizontals of the flesh, illustrious statesmen and bibulous mummers, cut-throats from Calabria and cut-purses from Jerusalem-atte-Bowe, Alsatia and Arcadia, monarchs, journalists, money-lenders, the famous and the infamous, all sitting amicably round the same table, hobnobbing, ex-changing amenities, offering up the same incense to the same false god.

Mentone is devoted to a gloomy piety and the adoration of ill-health.   There the residents are looked up to according to the acuteness of their maladies, those who are not consumptive do their best to simulate the symptoms, and those unfor-tunates, who find it impossible to conceal their robustness, are looked upon as outsiders and made to feel themselves outcasts.

Bordighera worships the Church and Stage.

Beaulieu and Nice are respectively English and French suburbs of Monte Carlo.

And thus I have summed up the whole of the Riviera.

Cannes, the close oligarchy, looks down upon it all, (democracy, aegrocracy—to coin a bastard word—and religion-and-water,) with thin contempt. The full vials of this are poured upon those strangers within its gates who are in it, but not of it. Mr. and Mrs. Wilfrid Tyrconnel were beginning to find themselves in this position.

When they first arrived, still honeymooning, they were acclaimed with open arms by the Pigeon's innumerable friends, who were most of them, more or less, members of the various sets that combine to form the governing class at Cannes during the winter. But his wife was unable to adapt herself to the tone of the place. Her strict views about right and wrong, descending to irritating details; her intolerance of the scarcely veiled humbug which goes to make up the conventions of society; her rooted antipathy to pleasure for pleasure's sake, to the whole spirit of hedonism, which is the keystone of life at Cannes, put her out of harmony with her surroundings and brought about incessant friction.

That peculiar hybrid, the Cannes young man, an invertebrate individual who poses as a person of light and leading in this second-rate colony and proses about his prowess at the golf-links or his luck at Monte Carlo, said that young Mrs. Tyrconnel gave herself airs—meaning that she snubbed him, which she did, unmercifully. The women took much the same tone.

Like all enthusiasts, Gwendolen was painfully deficient in tact. Had she not started a tirade against Monte Carlo, under the nose of the Grand-

Duchess, with some very unpleasant references to the bad example set by bigwigs who went there to play? Had not Lady Greyheather and the Hon. Mrs. Worrie come to call and found her surrounded by eleven chronic old maids, busy making stomachers for the deep sea fishermen, and had she not introduced everyone of these ill-favoured Parcæ and tried to force Lady Greyheather to take part in their humble revels over 'real English tea' cooked in a tin etna? Were there not a hundred and one new stories afloat about her eccentricities and outrageous assurance? Was she not the chief subject of conversation whenever the Vicomtesse Lepeigne had exhausted her usual stock of gossip with Madame Mufle at the Réunion, and when Miss Lyke-Spitelle waxed especially confidential with Frau Bachbyte? A good deal of this murmuring reached Gwendolen's ears, but she was of most Puritan obstinacy in her ethics and what she did was done almost as much from a distorted sense of humour as for conscience's sake.

The wedding had been boisterously quiet. That is to say, Gwendolen had insisted on its being absolutely quiet, and her aunt, while grudgingly acquiescing, had secretly done her utmost to make it as rampageous as possible. Gwendolen had 'views' about marriage. God forbid that she should consider it a sacrament, for she hated ritualism almost as much as she hated the Pope and the Devil,—two very real enemies in her psalm of life. But she claimed that it was a very sacred, holy thing, almost as sacred in its way as the Lord's Supper, wherein she took part every Sunday morning in her life. She did not invite herds of friends and acquaintances to watch her partake of that holy feast. Why then should they come to gape upon her on this other sacred occasion, when most of all a modest maiden would desire to be alone with her nearest and dearest? Her beloved old father to give her away and Wilfrid, her chosen one, to receive her;

Aunt Maria and the servants as witnesses; no bridesmaids, for, like most old heads on young shoulders, Gwendolen had few friends of her own age; and the solemn simple service in the old church of Grantchester, which she had known and loved so well from earliest infancy. That was her idea of a happy marriage,—a fit prelude to the happy life, of which, in her trustful innocence, she felt assured, so long as she did her duty.

Mrs. de Courcy Miles had had short patience when she heard these views enunciated. She had had visions of herself, clad in scarlet sammet, mystic, wonderful, flouncing up the aisle of Saint George's, Hanover-square, and exchanging familiar greetings with marquises and right honourables in the chancel, while Plantagenet-Unkels and the Overdone-Jones's sat and heard each other groan with jealousy in the dimmest recesses of the church. However, she knew it was no use arguing when once Gwendolen had made up her mind, so she agreed to a quiet wedding, and even to a quiet wedding at Cambridge, which was the hardest pill of any, and then set diligently to work to get hold of everybody whose name would look well in the *Post*.

In the event, Mrs. de Courcy Miles was woefully disappointed, for, at Gwendolen's request, Tyrconnel only asked his own immediate relatives and a few intimate friends. Coryton and his wife were away at Monte Carlo; Pimlico was laid up with influenza; Lady Giddy wouldn't come; Lady Elizabeth and Theodora were beyond her ken; Colonel Lockhart and Mr. Rupert Clifford disappointed her at the eleventh hour. So she had to be content with unaristocratic Lord Baltinglass and his dismal sister in the way of 'quality', Mr. Toadey-Snaile to represent the Legislature, the archdeaconess for the Church, and Sir Cincinnatus Spreadeagle for the Army, Navy and (more especially) the Reserve forces.

The Cambridge contingent of course mustered

in force, but they were of small account. The Vice-Chancellor officiated, assisted by Funnie-Ffoulkes and Professor Done-Brown of the woeful countenance. Belinda and Araminta donned new gowns for the occasion and twittered like a pair of canaries. Lady Catchbois brought out her old brocade and Mrs. Flummery-North appeared in a wondrous violet bonnet. Spofforth did full justice to the Professor's Champagne.

The honeymoon—like many honeymoons—had been a period of transition and disillusioning. Before three weeks were up, Gwendolen had realized that her husband was ineradicably wedded to the world and that not even her gentle influence would long be able to restrain him from returning to his old love for excitement. Tyrconnel for his part had discovered that even pure, flawless goodness palls after a time and that angelic beauty is only aggravating, when it is accompanied by copybook views of life.

The first time he was left alone for a couple of hours since his wedding—it was in Paris: she had gone to her dressmaker's and he to the Hammam—he had a good hard think about things in general and thought some very hard things about Gwendolen and his marriage in particular. Perhaps it was the luxurious atmosphere of the bath or the epicurean atmosphere of this Paris, which he knew and had enjoyed so well but was now no longer allowed to enjoy, that made him take French views of marriage and incompatibility of temper.

"She's too good for me, 'pon my word she is," he mused bitterly, as he watched the smoke of his cigarette curl up above his couch. "I really begin to sympathize with the Athenians, who got so tired of hearing Aristides called 'the Just,' that they drove him out of their city. I thought I was marrying a woman, but I find I have married an angel—and an angel is rather too much of a handful for a humble mortal like myself."

*

It had not come to any open quarrel yet, but Wilfrid had several times turned away impatiently, when Gwendolen pronounced her decision in her downright, uncompromising way, upon some minor point on which he had set his heart for the moment. At Paris she would not lunch at Voisin's nor dine at the Café Anglais, because they were 'too extravagant'; she would not go to the theatres, because they did not square with her notions of propriety; and as to going to hear Yvette Guilbert, she would as soon have thought of witnessing Miss Gussie Gutter's 'turn' at a palace of varieties in our own Leicester Square.

Now, as Tyrconnel ruefully asked himself in the cooling-room of the Turkish bath, if you don't eat good food and you don't see naughty plays and you don't hear Yvette Guilbert, where's the use of staying in Paris at all? When he thought over it less impatiently afterwards, he admitted to himself that he could not picture Gwen sitting

out '*Le Coquin de Printemps*' at the *Nouveautés*
or going into boisterous hilarity over '*Joséphine,
elle est malade*' or '*L'amour mouillé.*' So after a
few days, during which he vainly tried to interest
himself in the pictures at the Louvre and got
snubbed for suggesting a visit to the Morgue;
drove in a one-horse shay in the Bois; looked
into the shop windows at the Palais-Royal;
made pilgrimages to the Sainte-Chapelle and
the Eiffel tower: and dined at a Bouillon Duval:
he became anxious to move on and said so to
Gwendolen.

It was a great surprise to her and she was inclined
to remonstrate.

"Why!" she said, "you stipulated for at least
three weeks in Paris, which you said was the most
delightful place on earth. Now you want to hurry
me off, just as I am beginning to learn something
about the pictures too."

"Well, my dear," he replied, "the pictures can

wait till we return, and all our friends are on the Riviera.

"Oh! Wilfrid," she said in aggrieved tones, "are you so tired of me already that you want to get back to your friends? Besides we are not quite without friends. Mr. Rupert Clifford has asked us to go over to Saint-Germain on Thursday, and Aunt Maria and your Aunt Tyrconnel are to be here next week."

"That settles it. We absolutely must leave this week."

"But I specially wanted to wait for your Aunt Kezia. She promised to take me to the Gospel Temperance Mission, which her friend, Miss Mitten, is establishing in the *Quartier Latin.* You scamp," she added playfully, "I don't believe you want to see our good aunts a bit!"

"No, I do not," he replied with the very obvious compliment, to which she had been leading up; "at least not now. We have not been married so long

that we want intruders yet. I am sure Miss Mitten
will be glad to show you her mission-hall any day.
Nothing shall induce me to stay after this week.
The place is too outrageously dull."

"Dull!" Gwendolen gasped. She looked at him
with quivering lips for some moments, as if she
had received a blow in the face.

Tyrconnel was penitent at once.

"My darling!" he exclaimed eagerly; "you
know I didn't mean it like that. I could never be
really dull anywhere with you. But we may as
well be at a lively place as a dull one, and this
is enough to give anyone the blues."

"What! Paris? But you were so enthusiastic
about it before we came."

"Yes, but that was a different Paris. Don't
misunderstand me. I am quite willing not to go
to theatres and restaurants, if you think them
wrong, but you mustn't expect me to like plum-
cake so much, when all the plums are taken

out .... Dear, dear me! What is the matter?
Don't look at me with that pained, drawn expression,
as if I had uttered some blasphemy. I only live
for you now and we shall always be quite happy
so long as we love each other, as I pray we always
shall."

"You are very dear to me," she said softly,
taking his face between her hands and chastely
kissing his forehead, " but I sometimes wish you
were different in character. The old Adam dies
very hard in you yet."

" It will be all right some day, my good angel.
Meanwhile I would not have you differ one iota
from what God has made you. In my eyes you
are perfect as you are."

" Hush! Wilfrid dear," she said, looking into his
eyes with an air of infinite tenderness, and speaking
with more emotion than she often displayed, " there
is none perfect save One." And she pointed upward.

When his feelings were deeply stirred, Tyrconnel

felt this kind of ecstatic worship for his wife, but his moods soon passed and, as the weeks slipped by, they became rarer, while the contrary moods, when he repined at the weariness of his present life, became more frequent. He was proud to be good and true and he vowed to himself fifty times a day that nothing should make him swerve one hair's breadth from the narrow path. But the mental struggle and the constant murmuring, which found no outlet, as he rarely complained to Gwendolen and was too loyal to do so to anyone else,—these were telling on his health and temper.

While never particularly robust, he had not needed coddling or been considered delicate as a boy and had constantly led a healthy outdoor life. When he appeared at Cannes, everyone noticed that he stooped slightly and was pale and poorly to look at, and, when his old friends began to rally him upon it and tell him, as Pimlico brutally did on one occasion at the Beau-site, that evidently married life didn't agree with him, he was not slow in showing that he had replaced his lost good health by a newly-found bad temper, which they were quite unprepared for.

"I should advise raw beef-steaks every morning and a couple of dozen oysters the last thing at night," said Williams, putting on a consulting-room expression.

"Only not Mediterranean oysters," put in Wilmot, who of course was not far off. "You must get a barrel of Marennes from a man in the rue Saint-Honoré. I'll give you his address. Mediterranean oysters give you typhoid."

END OF VOL. II.